Desirable Aliens

ILLINOIS SHORT FICTION

Crossings by Stephen Minot
A Season for Unnatural Causes by Phillip F. O'Connor
Curving Road by John Stewart
Such Waltzing Was Not Easy by Gordon Weaver

Rolling All the Time by James Ballard
Love in the Winter by Daniel Curley
To Byzantium by Andrew Fetler
Small Moments by Nancy Huddleston Packer

One More River by Lester Goldberg
The Tennis Player by Kent Nelson
A Horse of Another Color by Carolyn Osborn
The Pleasures of Manhood by Robley Wilson, Jr.

The New World by Russell Banks
The Actes and Monuments by John William Corrington
Virginia Reels by William Hoffman
Up Where I Used to Live by Max Schott

The Return of Service by Jonathan Baumbach
On the Edge of the Desert by Gladys Swan
Surviving Adverse Seasons by Barry Targan
The Gasoline Wars by Jean Thompson

Desirable Aliens by John Bovey
Naming Things by H. E. Francis
Transports and Disgraces by Robert Henson
The Calling by Mary Gray Hughes

DESIRABLE ALIENS

Stories by John Bovey

UNIVERSITY OF ILLINOIS PRESS

Urbana Chicago London

Manufactured in the United States of America

"The Stroke of Twelve," *Carleton Miscellany,* vol. 16, nos. 1 & 2, Fall-Winter, 1976–1977

"The Garden Wall," *Ploughshares,* vol. 4, no. 2, 1978; *Iron,* no. 26, September-November, 1979 (U.K.)

"The Tigers of Wrath," *Virginia Quarterly Review,* vol. 54, no. 2, Spring, 1978

"The Lady of Shalott," *Cornhill Magazine,* no. 1079, Spring, 1974 (U.K.); *Four Quarters,* vol. 29, no. 4, Summer, 1980

"The Bigger Thing," *Blackwood's Magazine,* vol. 324, no. 1955, September, 1978 (U.K., under title "Julian"); *Foreign Service Journal,* vol. 53, no. 9, September, 1976.

"Concert," *Kansas Quarterly,* vol. 6, no. 1, Winter, 1973–74

"The Sign of the Horns," *Carleton Miscellany,* vol. 18, no. 2, 1980; *Paris Voices,* no. 3, Autumn, 1978 (France)

"The Furies," *Literary Review,* vol. 20, no. 2, Winter, 1977; *Paris Voices,* no. 5, Summer, 1979 (France)

"Famous Trials," *New England Review,* vol. 2, no. 3, Spring, 1980; *Stand,* vol. 21, no. 2, March, 1980 (U.K.)

"The Overlap," *Canto,* vol. 3, no. 3, Summer, 1980

Library of Congress Cataloging in Publication Data

Bovey, John, 1913-
  Desirable aliens.

  (Illinois short fiction)
  I. Title.
PZ4.B7822De [PS3552.0843]   813'.54   80-18596
ISBN   0-252-00837-5   (cloth)
ISBN   0-252-00838-3   (paper)

For Marcia

Contents

Ah! que le monde est grand à la clarté des lampes!
Aux yeux du souvenir que le monde est petit!

—Baudelaire, "Le Voyage"

The Stroke of Twelve

Of wartime Halifax the misted lense recaptures first of all the ice-rutted streets, the brown snow, the gray penurious indifferent town, closing its eyes tight, tight, against the horde of outlanders—British, American, Canadian—who pass and repass from ship to shore, from shore to ship, jamming the liquor stores and the lobby of the Lord Nelson Hotel, drinking and whoring, sighing with relief or shrinking from visions of death by fire and death by freezing. Over everything in Halifax hovers the expectation of catastrophe in the Arctic reaches that lie only a day's voyage to the northeast.

Even for Captain MacDermott, U.S.N., and the four reservists ("the ensigns" he calls us, lumping us together, as one might say "the kids") who share with him the opprobrium of duty on shore, the horizons of Halifax rarely brighten. I see again the chattering teletypes in the Convoy Office; I hear the shrill beeping of the radios and the hooting of corvettes beyond the frosted windows. And the voices: the sardonic growl of Captain Mac; the curses of Hal and Ted as they nursemaid our antique coding machine, which we have dubbed the Spinning Jenny; the fresh tones of Eliot, youngest and most obliging, the darling of the cipher girls. And then I hear, at first just faintly, the voice of Helen, with its Nova Scotian burr, and the viewfinder begins to clear.

Deplorable though my civilian ways might be, the Captain sensed that my twenty-six years had given me a worldly ease that the younger ensigns, for all their starched collars and gleaming shoes, had yet to develop. Until they did, he assigned me to be meeter and greeter. I trotted from wardroom to wardroom with mail and bottles and sealed orders; I escorted bored admirals through the bureaucratic maze of the dockyard; I tried to homogenize green ensigns of the Armed Guard with the seadogs who captained their freighters. In moments of zeal, not unrelated to the quarterly fitness ratings, I invited Francie, the eldest and homeliest of the Captain's daughters, to mingle with the *jeunesse dorée* of Halifax at the "rat races." (During these dances I was expected to protect her chastity from the wolves who roamed the corridors of the Admiralty House, although Francie let me understand that my devotion to duty was excessive.) But the most ungrateful chore was meeting the trains from Boston. I had to be on the platform whenever they brought in convoy officers or the civil servants who tested underwater weapons in the Minas Basin. Snows often delayed the trains: I spent many nights stamping up and down the grimy sheds of the Halifax station. It was there that I met Helen.

The November night had driven me from the wind-swept platform into the waiting room. I ordered a pallid cup of coffee (there were no bars in Halifax) to warm my fingers back to life. Then I settled on one of the yellow oak benches with *Pride and Prejudice*, but intellectual snobbery failed to keep me upright on the slippery seat, and the Bennets didn't come across very well in that dingy vault, with its smells of soot and spoiled fruit. I put down my book and gave myself up to the anonymous signals of transit: girls in shabby sealskin flicking by on pipestem legs in search of their mates; sailors with their silly ribboned hats and their shouldered duffle bags, swinging along on their way to unknown destinations—perhaps to death and disaster, which I would presently convert into statistics for the teletypes.

A stifled whimper startled me. At the other end of my bench a girl sat huddled in a sheepskin coat, her stocking cap pushed back on shining, reddish hair, with bangs straggling over her forehead. She stared ahead at nothing; her hands were spread limply, palms out, against the edge of the seat. An exhausted skier, one would have said, except that, as I watched, a tear trickled down her cheek.

Even the promiscuities of the Lord Nelson hadn't made me very enterprising with strange girls, and certainly not with weepers. She was so muffled up that I couldn't make out her figure, and at first I hardly noticed her features—just the shining hair and the slow tears, and then her long, trembling fingers. But I heard my own voice; it sounded disembodied, involuntary: "Are you in trouble?"

The question was not intelligent. But when I repeated it, she thrust out her lower lip and nodded, like a child overcome with humiliation. "I'd not be worse off dead," she said softly.

I inched closer. Mechanically I asked if she had lost anyone: bad news was frequent in those days. Even though she shook her head, I persisted. "Someone in the Navy maybe?"

She clasped her hands. "I've lost no one."

I couldn't stop there. In the space of minutes, the distress that hung all around me in Halifax had ceased to be vicarious: I had captured a direct S.O.S. I wanted desperately to hold the circuit open.

At her feet I noticed a little overnight satchel of green cloth in a paisley design, with scuffed plastic edges and a tag dangling from its handle, on which was inked "Gardiner."

"Are you going away?"

Her eyes flickered speculatively, but without impatience, from my brass buttons to the eagle above my visor. She fished a crumpled ball of handkerchief from the pocket of her sheepskin. "I canna decide." She mopped at her cheeks. "I'm thinking I haven't the guts." "Goots," she pronounced it. The word rang false: her voice was youthful, gentle, unsuited to borrowed roughness.

"Guts to do what? Are you thinking of going to sea?"

She colored a little at my dryness but managed a smile. "Sounds bloody silly, I suppose, but I'd go almost anywhere if it would do any good."

"Ah, you're in love then."

This was a leap forward all right—perhaps into a gulf. But she didn't refuse it. "If that was all," she said, with an edge of scorn, "I mought get over it."

I reached out to touch her arm. "Tell me what it's all about. It might help—for a minute or two anyway."

"Oh, there's others have offered to take my mind off my troubles." She looked around wildly, as though I had backed her into a corner. "I found out soon enough what they meant. I canna stay here anyway. Naught I can do. Nor you."

I must have looked rather chilled by this shower of Nova Scotian negatives, because she added, "Thanks anyway."

"Thanks for what?"

"Well now, for feeling sorry, I guess."

We both got up. She had blue-green eyes, widely spaced and bright, though the lids were swollen with weeping; a wide, gentle mouth; a few freckles, startling in a complexion of winter pallor. The beaten-up coat didn't reveal much, but she had a straight ease of bearing, a posture of modesty that trembled on the edge of pride.

"Let me ask you something." I spoke fast, as though she might dissolve before my eyes in the stale air of the station. "If you were sure I was offering help just to be—well, just to be helpful, that's all—would you still give me the brush-off?"

"But there's naught to brush off. At least not between you and me."

I scrambled for my wallet and found a calling card. "You can get me at the Lord Nelson. Just let me know if you get to feeling too lousy. That's all. Honestly."

She looked at the card with a faint astonishment, and then, with a shrug, she slipped it into her pocket. She picked up her sad little bag. I raised my hand to my visor, and off she went without a backward glance.

I stood there holding that vacant salute, like a man who has forgotten to close his umbrella inside a building. And then I heard the chuffing of the Boston train and the squeak of brakes.

In the time that followed I thought of her often. But ten days went by, and even in Halifax there were distractions. The surveillance of convoys meant that the teletype and code room had to be manned every minute. Tardiness was a cardinal sin. Captain MacDermott wasted no breath on landlubbers, but late appearances had earned me a curt threat: how would I like to ship out on a freighter carrying ammo and explosives to Murmansk? "Easily arranged," he told me. "No waiting lines."

The algebra of staggered watches produced strange equations of duty and leisure. One evening I might snatch a half-hour at the jangly piano in the hotel's empty ballroom; the next evening I might be bent over the keyboard of the Spinning Jenny in the code room. Pink gins at Admiralty House or sieges of the dockyard's demi-vierges might fall in mid-morning or at midnight. Only the Captain's daughter quarreled with this erratic system: fun-loving Francie pouted when we deserted her at dances or hauled her away from the ski slope. The Captain had never set her straight, and she laid our defections to inconstancy or bad planning.

One morning I came into the hotel from night watch to find in my box a flannelly pink envelope with no stamp. The note had no salutation. "I wonder do you remember me? I'll wait at six o'clock tonight, the same place. Helen Gardiner." The writing was large, boldly slanting, but straggly, as though set down in a moving vehicle.

I had the duty at six, but Eliot, who worried about my celibacy, swapped hours with a wink.

Helen was sitting on the same bench in her sheepskin, her bag at her feet. She raised her eyes to my buttons and then dazedly to my face. "Thanks for coming." No tears, but her voice was suffocated.

I took her by the elbow and guided her across the street as though she had been blind. We found a coffee bar where, if we couldn't get a drink, we had at least the privacy of a booth. Helen held her cup in her left hand, curling the gloved fingers of her right as if frostbitten.

She flushed at my glance. "It's nothing. A little accident. With a piano, would you believe?"

"A piano! What in God's name—? Here, let me see."

She shook her head and put her hand in her lap. "It's no great thing. Just the keyboard cover that fell."

Hot coffee acted like a potion: her troubles came tumbling out. She spread them before me unembroidered, and her low voice with its whispers of Scots, gave to their banality the accents of legend.

Her father had been a civil servant all his life, a gray bureaucrat, I gathered, who had accepted detachment to the Navy for the duration, mainly for the extra pay. Her mother had died suddenly the summer the war broke out.

"It's only three years ago," Helen said, "and already it's another world."

"War changes things fast."

"I don't mean the war so much. It's other things. Dad married again right off. A Canuck from Restigouche. Lost her husband in the Caribbean just after she came down to Halifax. There they were—both lonely—and she with two girls on her hands. They're older than me."

"Still that must be some help."

"Help!" Her voice caught in a bitter little laugh. "Hate me, they do. All three of them, from the word go. Not a decent word in the whole three years."

"What about your father?"

"He loves me right enough, Dad does. That's the trouble. But he's never there—bouncing all over Canada for the Navy. And he canna bear the womenfolk screeching. But he worries about me—and I about him. He's not been well; he comes back tired, and he looks so yellow. So when he's home, I leave the talebearing and all to the others."

"It's like Cinderella."

"Cinderella is it?" Her bright eyes looked into mine and then dropped. The parallel did not amuse her. "If you like"—and with a glimmer of malice: "But I canna see Prince Charming anywhere about."

When her father was away, she drugged herself with movies or wandered about on the Citadel, where, she let me know with a certain archness, her tears hadn't always kept the sailors away.

A dozen times she had got to the verge of leaving home for good. She would count her pennies and pack her bag. She had got to know the departure boards at the station by heart: Lunenburg, Yarmouth, Moncton, St. John. "And then there's the big time, you know: Toronto, Montreal, Boston."

But the prospect of being alone and broke in those strange, cold places made her shrink back. And there was her father. So she crawled back to the shingle-plated duplex in Barrington Street—there were dozens of them, standing mournfully cheek by jowl—and nursed her defeat in her room.

Sometimes she checked the paisley bag at the station, like a hostage for escape. But one morning her stepmother had caught her on the stairs with it.

"'Well now, where have we been?' says she. And she gives me a dirty smile and says she'll pray for me."

"Pray for you?"

"Oh, madly devout she is. R.C. and priest-ridden. The girls too. But I just laughed at her, and she told me to keep the bag handy for my travels. Said it would be good riddance to us both."

"And what about the piano?"

"I have a go now and then, when the others are out of the house. An old upright—belonged to my mother."

"Why not take lessons?"

"Now wouldn't I love that!" She brightened. "I'm not too bad you know. And then there's the big conservatories—Toronto or even Montreal. But of course my stepmother won't hear of Dad spending the money. When he's away she keeps me from the piano."

"How?"

"Talking and carrying on while I'm playing. And then the girls: the eldest tries to play. Last night they made an awful row. We got into a regular fight and they slammed the cover."

She drew off her glove and held up her hand. The middle fingers were bruised purple; one of the nails was black underneath.

Helen had flung out of the house and walked the icy streets to the Dartmouth ferry. Four crossings she had made, staring into the great dark basin. In the morning hours she had gone home and scrawled the note and brought it to the hotel.

Groping for a lifeline to throw her, I told her about the Steinway in the hotel and my own strumming. The faint coal of her confidence brightened, and presently, when I had piled conversational kindling around it, a tongue of flame appeared. It turned out that both of us went for "classical" rather than jazz. She preferred Brahms to Schumann; with me, the opposite. And so we kept things moving until I looked at my watch: an hour had passed. Eliot would be waiting for me.

Ten days later, she wrote again. This time I had the afternoon free, and I got to the coffee bar before she did. The paisley bag was missing; my hopes rose. They fell again when she said, "My dad's come home to stay. He'll not be going on any more trips. He's very ill."

"Not much luck in your family. What's wrong?"

"Cancer, the doctor tells us."

"Us" was a new note. No question of her going away then. Unworthily, my heart gladdened. "Look," I said, "I don't go much for this dump. And you know me well enough by now to come over to the hotel. Nothing to be afraid of."

"No, of course not." I wasn't much flattered by this, especially when she added, "I should love a good cup of tea."

All the same, she was intimidated by the Lord Nelson's carpets and chandeliers and by the officers' uniforms. In one corner a contingent of Armed Guard lieutenants, fresh from New York and bound for Greenock, were circulating a bottle ostentatiously under the table. Their noise stopped as we passed. One of them recognized me from the Convoy Office. He smiled but his thoughts were clear: the shoregoing Navy—all of the booze and the bimboes and none of the nitty-gritty.

I took Helen's arm in mine. "Do you really want tea?"

"That would be lovely." But as we passed the ballroom door, the grand piano caught her eye. She looked at me, and her freckles shone.

"It's all right. Try it if you want."

"I'll not be disturbing anyone?"

"No one. Unless maybe you do the 'Polonaise Militaire.' "

She laughed softly—it was the first time—and crossed the ballroom, gliding stealthily as though the floor might give way under her. She had long, pretty legs. When I took her coat, I saw that her breasts, under her thick jersey, were bigger than I had expected.

She began with the E-Major Étude of Chopin. I could see that she was no concert artist: no bravura about her. She just played in the same way she had told her troubles: I could see her emotions through plate glass. And I saw my own. The rising melancholy of the Étude carried me away from Halifax: I was back home at the family piano with its creaking pedal. A rush of warmth; my eyes filled.

Helen did the "Minute Waltz," a bit unsteadily, and then—remembering, I'm sure, about me and Schumann—the "Prophet Bird." She closed the piano after that and stood very straight beside it.

"I've never enjoyed anything more," I told her.

"Really now?"

"Really." I added hoarsely, "Why not come up to the room for a little while?"

"No. No, I don't want that. Not now. Maybe never."

"Never? Don't you want love, Helen?"

"How would I know it was love? I've not had all that much."

But before she went away—alone once again—she reached up and gently stroked my cheek.

In the days that followed she wrote no more but came herself, making my crazy hours even crazier. "A young lady in the lobby, sir." And I would go down to find her bolt upright on a sofa, under the puzzled eye of the desk clerk, whose experience of the military had not prepared him for the enigma of our chastity.

Sometimes we took turns at the piano, or we just sat and talked about the war or her father's illness. One morning I stumbled in after a tough night on the circuit—we had received a flash about the North African landings—and sat with Helen in the lobby. In the middle of giving her the news, I fell asleep with her hand in mine—an odd sight no doubt. When I awoke, she was gone.

One Saturday I asked Helen to the "rat race" at Admiralty House, juggling hours so as to have the whole night off. I had decided to advance my lines beyond the beachhead I had so carefully staked out.

Helen's party dress was one of her daytime jerseys, tricked out with an artificial gardenia at the waist. She wore long, pearl-drop earrings that bobbled about when we danced. She was graceful and quick to follow, but she scowled under the glare of the electric globes and fidgeted at the music ("It's bloody loud") and the drunken voices rising in waves around us. When I introduced her to Francie MacDermott and her circle, eyebrows rose perceptibly all around.

At midnight I fetched our coats and telephoned for a taxi. We waited, arm in arm, under the glass marquee, and when the taxi came, I directed the driver to the Lord Nelson and started to climb in after her.

She laid her fingers timidly on my wrist. "I'm sorry, but it's straight home for me tonight."

"You can't even come up for a drink?"

"They'll be fretting."

"They, them! Let them fret, for Christ's sake."

"No, really I canna. Not with Dad lying there. But many thanks."

"Thanks for nothing!"

"I mean for the dance and all."

My mouth was dry with anger: I saw all those carefully arranged hours stretching blankly ahead. "Better hurry," I said, "or your coach will turn into a pumpkin." But still I held the door open.

"I hate it when you talk like that."

"You do, do you?"

"It makes everything false—secondhand, like we were play-acting."

"It's a way I have. Anyway, we are, aren't we?"

"Are what now?"

"Playacting."

"Well, I hate it. I'm no Cinderella. Or Rachmaninoff. Or anybody else but Helen Gardiner. Nor like to be."

"Okay, okay," the driver shouted. "Let's pack it up, wee ones."

Helen slammed the door and off they went, but not before I had yelled after them, "Watch out for those white mice!"

The new year crawled upward from the longest nights and, after Guadalcanal, from the darkest of our days. But not for Helen. One evening the desk clerk called in panic: would I come down right away?

I found Helen sobbing in a corner of the lobby. My reaction was not noble: if she sat there blubbering away in front of strangers or Eliot and the other ensigns, they would think only one thing. And God knew how wide of the mark they would be! I took her firmly, angrily, by the elbow and steered her to the elevator. I got her safely into my room, too dazed to object, and she threw herself facedown on my bed. I sat on the edge and stroked her hair, with now and then an ineffectual pat on the shoulder. After a bit she sat up and dabbed at her eyes. I brought her a cold washcloth; she buried her face in it.

She told me what I had guessed. "Hopeless now," she said. "Hopeless. It goes so fast these days—but not fast enough for him. Poor Dad! Whatever can I do, my God? And then afterwards—"

I wondered that she hadn't seen it coming; maybe her father's illness had shifted the pattern of her ordeal too sharply. But now the last barrier was giving way.

"I'll have no one. Already there's no one really. You'll have to help me."

"Of course I will." I didn't see how, but what could I say?

She reached for my hand. "You're so bloody decent. And me so bloody prissy."

"Prissy?"

"The last time—after the dance."

"Don't worry about it."

"And before. All the help, and you asking so little. I canna believe it."

My hand went a bit cold in hers. I had kept my word all right. And I had ended by needing her because in Halifax, where emergencies and victories always belonged to someone else, she was the only one who needed me. But how to explain anything so meager?

"You've got dearer to me than I ever thought," she said. "Without you, I mought have killed myself." Still I could find nothing to say. "There now. Don't you believe me?"

"Okay. Sure, I believe you."

"Oh, there's more to it than that. Much more." And then almost without transition: "If you still want me, that is."

I pulled my hand away from hers, and her pale face went all ablaze: she had misunderstood my surprise. "I'll not be pushing myself at you. Not for the world. If you dinna feel the same, well, there it is. But"—she hesitated—"I'm thinking I love you. And yet it's funny: I still canna quite tell."

I touched her ear and her cheek with my lips. Then she threw her arms around my neck and closed her eyes and put her mouth frantically to mine. My arms went around her, and we fell across the bed. Her cheek was wet on mine.

A little timidly she helped my fingers with her clothes. At the back of my mind, like a trickle of icy water, ran the thought of the sailors on the Citadel. But when her sobs passed over into sighs, I knew that all that didn't matter for either of us. "Dear God, oh God," she moaned, and I thrust myself upon her as though her life depended on me.

After that she came whenever I was off watch. Sometimes this was in the afternoon as in the first days, but the piano in the ballroom stayed shut. What we both hated most was the cold, gray morning when we straggled through the lobby under the eye of the desk clerk. But the Lord Nelson was the center of our life: Helen never allowed me to take her farther than the taxi stand. Twice I heard her direct the driver to the hospital.

One evening she didn't show up.

I sat late in the lobby, pretending to read the papers. The next day I drove back from the dockyard at lunchtime to see if she had left word. There was nothing. And how could I help now? I wouldn't be welcome in Barrington Street. I couldn't wander up and down those rows of blankly staring houses on the gamble of running into her. By the weekend I was sick with longing.

On Monday I came off watch bone-tired. The first Soviet submarine had arrived from Coco Solo under U.S. escort. I had spent the hours from midnight to dawn passing messages from Washington to suspicious and drunken Russian officers. Back in my room, I peeled off my uniform and crawled into bed in my skivvies. And then a gentle knocking pulled me away from the edge of sleep.

Helen wore no mourning and assumed no funeral airs. She stood in the doorway, straight as an arrow, smiling shyly, her hair tousled under her cap. Her eyes were rimmed with red, but I saw that this time tears had refreshed her; there was grief in her face, but no despair.

I sat her down by the window and gave her a shot glass of Bourbon. I asked what I could do.

She sipped at the whisky, making a wry face. "Well, luv"—it was the first time she had used that endearment, as if to a child—"you mought start by putting on your bathrobe." Her blue-green eyes glinted; she sounded almost perky. "No, really there's naught more anyone can do. Quite peaceful it was: a coma at the end. Funeral was yesterday. Very simple: no announcements." She gave a long sigh. "Oh, but it's so glad I am. For him, I mean. And I reckon for me too."

"What about your stepmother?"

"She hasn't been too bad, you know. She called in the priest of course, but no harm done. It's rather hard lines for her—twice widowed and all. But with the two girls, she'll draw a good pension. I'm glad for that too. And anyway my dad has left a bit of money. As he made no will, they tell me I'll have a good part. No one can touch it either."

"That's great, Helen."

I sat on the arm of her chair, and she drew me down for a kiss. There was none of the fire or the tumult of the past weeks, and when she drew away again, she looked anxious. I sensed that the last days had brought a turn of the wheel.

"I'm going away, luv," she said finally. "I'm leaving Halifax."

"Leaving?" I groped for a quip to pace my recovery. "Where's your green bag?"

"Oh, it's not like that any more. I shall have a go at the conservatory in Toronto. I've enough to cover me for a year, if I'm careful."

"So you've found the guts to do it."

She looked up, startled: her ear had caught the bitter edge of my recollection. "Shall you mind?"

"What do you think? Of course I'll mind."

"I suppose it all sounds silly."

What did it matter how it sounded? What did the world's opinion matter? She must—she couldn't not, really—have a try. One of these days I should be moving on myself, maybe to sea. I probably wouldn't turn out to be a virtuoso either.

"It's not silly, Helen. It's the only thing for you. And don't be all that careful either."

"You're sweet, luv. I'll not forget you. Never."

"You said never once before."

"I remember."

"Never is a big deal."

"Not for me it isn't." She chuckled as I got up. "How could I ever forget you standing there in that bloody old bathrobe."

If I had batted an eyelash right then, she would have leaped up, quick as fire. But she would be making amends. I might want her again, but I didn't want that. No, by God. Even though she might set sail on her own, I was the one—passing her way by chance maybe, but still it was I—who had lifted her over the bar.

When I peered through the window, I saw the bare branches dripping in the brown light. For the first time I heard ice shifting on the roof and then a muffled thud on the sidewalk. The winter was dying.

I tossed the maligned bathrobe on the bed and started climbing back into my blues. "Today I'll take you home—and in a U.S. Navy jeep—all the way to your door."

She didn't answer, and for a minute I thought she was angry. Then she said calmly, "All the way, eh? Well, why not, luv? Yes, I shouldn't mind at all."

Knotting my tie before the mirror, I watched her in the armchair. And I saw everything in Halifax—the bald streets; the rows of racing teletypes; the faces of the Captain, of Francie, of the ensigns, even of Helen, as her foot adjusted to the glass slipper—everything in the eye of memory.

But that dashing officer in the mirror—where did he fit in?

I was young. I still trusted in my pact with the universe. I should get through the war all right. But among the thousands of persons of my lifetime, I would not love again in quite the same way as I had loved before.

The Garden Wall

The air at the bottom of the garden was damp, but when Cecilia Lofton opened the gate, a gust of the *chergui*, loaded with needles of hot sand, struck her in the face. Raising her hand defensively, she squinted down the dusty road that meandered among scrubby palms and shacks of tin and cardboard until it was lost in the summer bronze of the plain. In the distance the white mass of Casablanca wavered in the heat. The blue-green overscoring of the ocean was like a promise of far-off happiness.

Just as she ducked back into the cool of the garden, Cecilia noticed the break in the wall. A long fissure ran jaggedly along the base, with smaller cracks splaying out from it into the moss-stained concrete. She could see nothing like it anywhere else in the white-washed ramparts that sealed her off from neighbors farther up the hill. But the autumn rains might start at any moment, and if the base crumbled, the terraced lawn would begin to go too. When Colonel Lofton returned from the south, he would be vexed. And when their landlord came back from France, he would blame his American tenants.

"It must be this weird climate," said Cecilia aloud to no one. "First the drought and then the damp—and now both." A minor mishap really; why should she be so dismayed?

Since Titus would be away with the French at Ben Guerir until autumn was well along, she decided to phone Jake Copps at the Engineers' Section of the airbase. Majors were created to help

colonels and their wives: no need to be squeamish about the con-
veniences of rank.

The Major, in approved army style, yearned to set things right.
"You couldn't have picked a better moment. We've got a lot of
indigènes over here in the manpower pool just sitting on their—well, I
mean there's not much for them to do, now that we've finished the
second airstrip."

"You've got a lot of what, Jake?"

"Natives, Mrs. Lofton. Ayrabs. Most of them will hang around
until the rains begin, hoping for more U.S. gravy."

"I hadn't thought of our wall as gravy. Can you really send them
all the way out here for it?"

"They'll snap at it. I might even scratch up a real mason or two.
You may need to keep an eye on them: things are a bit sensitive with
the French right now, and for the Moroccans, the Americans are no
different. If you have problems, just give me a buzz. But of course
you've got the two boys there. And the neighbors."

Cecilia gave a little shuddering laugh, rising to the challenge like a
good army wife. "The boys are at camp in France. And the neighbors—well, you know after two years in this place, I haven't the
faintest idea who they are. But I don't think the nationalists are
going to take their revenge out on me."

Jake Copps laughed too, but a little uncomfortably. "I'll ask the
Bureau to send along a Frenchman. It's a shade irregular, but your
place is a little off the beaten path. That way the work will get done
faster too."

"I don't want you violating any treaties for me, Jake."

"Break the rules for you any day," said the Major. "We'll just
chalk it up to buildings and grounds."

"You're an angel, Jake."

But after Cecilia had hung up, she still felt uneasy. Had she
turned her garden wall into an international incident?

2

The familiar olive-drab truck, with the Engineers' turret blazoned
on its door, stood in the driveway when Cecilia got back from the

market. The *chergui* had brought staggering heat, but the work party had apparently gone straight to the job. In all her years as army daughter and army wife, Cecilia had never failed to marvel at this alacrity, even when she was depressed by many of its results.

Her first glimpse from the terrace, however, gave her something of a shock. Jack Copps's brisk efficiency had reduced her expectations to scale: rather than a group of burnoosed Arabs, the work party consisted of just two men. The Frenchman wore no uniform—he was apparently a *cochon de civil*—and no emblem of the protecting nation. He squatted under a fig tree, chewing on a cigar and staring listlessly at a bed of carnations. Cecilia took an instant dislike to his fat, red neck and to the sun helmet that bobbed on his head like an article of costume.

The other man stood in the flowerbed, exploring with his hands the moss-covered foundation of the wall. He was bent over so that at first Cecilia saw only an Arab skullcap and an expanse of blue shirt, badly torn, and soiled American dungarees. When he stood up, she made out a face that was olive-skinned and hawk-nosed, with sharply grooved demarcations, visible even from the terrace.

The man looked up and his eyes met hers. His appraisal was half-sensual, half-mocking; she felt at once the Moslem contempt for women. The religion of young men didn't interest Cecilia, but she was not used to such candor; even at forty, an American officer's wife was not a *fatma* or a beast of burden. She hesitated for a minute at the terrace railing. She could either descend into the full blaze of encounter, or retreat—with composure, of course—to the house. Finally she grasped the balustrade and marched down into the garden.

She stopped on the last step, turning her back on the Arab just below, and motioned to the Frenchman, who had got up from the shade of the fig tree. He shambled toward her, revolving his helmet in his hand.

"You come from the Engineers' office, monsieur?" Her French, at such junctures, never flowed quite as she hoped.

"Oui, madame."

"Where are the rest of the workmen?"

"There are no more, madame."

"I see." Behind her she heard the clink of metal and then a rhythmic tapping at the wall. "Well, at least this one seems to know what he's to do."

The Frenchman rubbed his pitted chin. "Oh, you have luck, madame. This one is a trained mason. Commandant Copps said I was to tell you that."

The tapping stopped suddenly. "Perhaps," said Cecilia, "he understands English as well as masonry."

The Frenchman's jaw dropped as he took in this new facet of the enterprise. "Really, madame, I couldn't say. We speak only French together."

"Well, let's find out. What is his name?"

"My name is Meknassy," said the voice behind her; its tone was flat and shallow. "And I speak English—oh, I speak it well."

Cecilia wheeled and lost her footing on the step. A wiry hand grasped her wrist and held it until she stood safely on the flagstones below. She flushed with the irritation of an unwilling beneficiary and smoothed a strand of hair into place. The back of her hand was wet. "Thank you," she said, "or should it be *merci?* Or perhaps *barak allah houfik?*"

The Arab looked at her as though she were baiting a trap. "As you wish, as you wish. If the American lady really speak Arabic—" He gave her a flash of gold teeth. "But maybe English will be best. I know the Americans already from before."

"From before?"

"From ten years ago. The landings, you know."

"Ah, the landings." She hardly knew where to go from there. Linguistically, she had been taken down a peg. Or maybe Meknassy hoped to enlist her complicity against his French warden, who stood by, scratching his head. Whatever the gambit, Cecilia decided to accept it. In carefully mouthed English, as though the Moroccan were deaf, she explained what she wanted. Nothing drastic, she told him, just a patch so that the wall would hold up through the rains.

Meknassy listened impassively, his brown arms folded across his chest, his long fingers grasping the trowel. On closer view, the man's head was disappointing. For all their primitive clarity, his features were lopsided. One side of his face—eye socket, cheekbone, jaw—

was a shade lower than the other, as though his head had been squeezed in some slow, relentless vise. The vise of poverty, Cecilia thought. Not even the sheen of his youth could conceal the guile and cruelty that poverty produced; they were already etched in the corners of his mouth and eyes. As a girl, she had seen such faces among poor whites.

When she had completed her little exercise in the psychology of command, Meknassy eyed her with scorn. *"Tout ce que tu me dis,"* he said, *"je le savais déjà."*

Cecilia flushed. When she gave no answer, the Frenchman said, "If you wish, madame, perhaps I can explain what you want."

"You don't think I am capable of handling the situation?"

"I was only trying to help you, madame."

"No help needed. And please put your helmet on. You'll have a sunstroke."

The Moroccan observed her outburst with a smile. But Cecilia's cup had run over. Again in English, she said, "Since you already know all there is to know, perhaps you'd better get on with it. The faster you finish, the better—for everyone."

The man touched his skullcap, spread his hand across his chest in a parody of the Arab blessing, and doubled over in a bow. "Bravo! *Barak allah houfik!"* he cried.

As she climbed stiffly up the steps, Cecilia heard the two of them snickering together.

3

Cecilia resolved that she would not go near the wall again until her advice was asked. But for three days she had to endure, morning and afternoon, the steady chopping of the pick. On Tuesday she escaped to the base hospital, where it was her day to help out, and in the evening the director of the constructors' consortium gave a cocktail party.

Some penitential instinct made Cecilia prolong her chores at the hospital, and then, stifling her desire to return to her garden, she went directly to the cocktail party, where she stayed well beyond the hour expected even of the Colonel's wife. When she got back to the villa, she found Manuela, the Spanish cook, muttering over the state of her solitary dinner. The garden was empty—she could see a pile of rubble in the corner—and the tools were neatly stacked by the steps. Cecilia felt a pang of disappointment, as though she had endured the tedium of official charity and official amusement, only to be cheated of her just compensation.

Wednesday was worse. Household duties seemed to draw her more and more often to the windows of the salon; the shutters were closed against the heat, but when she peered down through the slits, she could see the foreman's white helmet and the Moroccan's pick, flashing in long arcs. And then she saw that Manuela and the house-boy were keeping watch on her comings and goings. Unless she called Jake Copps and cancelled the whole project, she would have no peace.

She had lifted the phone to dial the base when she realized that Major Copps would find her request incomprehensible, even fantastic. With the rhythm of the pick in her ears, she couldn't say that his man was soldiering on the job. And she could well imagine Titus's reaction if he returned to find nothing but a great hole in the wall. He would push her caprices aside as if with a bulldozer. "You should have made them finish the job, Cissy. Copps stretched a point to help us. If the native acted up, it was up to the Frenchman to set him straight."

Just then the sound of the pick stopped.

Cecilia waited briefly, and when the silence continued, she put down the phone. Opening the terrace shutters with a clatter, she went quickly down the garden steps.

A huge gash yawned from the top to the bottom of the wall. The garden lay open to the stares of the Arabs who padded barefoot along the dusty road, and chunks of concrete were strewn over the parterre. Meknassy triumphed among the ruins, stirring cement ferociously in a trough, pausing now and then to slick the sweat from his forehead.

The foreman had retired to the shade of his fig tree, out of the range of flying fragments. He peered sullenly at her from under his helmet, shifting on his haunches to get up; when she passed him by, he sank back, offended, to the rumination of his cigar.

Cecilia addressed the Moroccan: "You've certainly done a lot of work." This admission did not mask her real meaning: a fine hash you've made of my wall.

The Moroccan looked her up and down before he answered. "Your wall was not good," he said in English. His insolence lay just under the surface. "But it will be okay now. You will see. New bottom part—everything from ground up. That is the way to build."

The didactic note made her smile. Where had he picked up that line? "What part of Morocco do you come from?"

"From Meknès." He leaned over to dredge cement from his trough. "That is what my name means: Meknassy."

"But what are you doing in Casablanca?"

"I come when the Americans come—the first time." And he told her that at the time of the landings, he was too young for any military service, but in the general effervescence, he had left home to pick up a little money working in the port. Afterward there was nothing to go back to in Meknès. "I am no grocer like my father. From the Americans I learn new things: driving trucks; fixing them; cooking. Masonry too."

"Is your family still in Meknès then?"

"My father only. Mother and brother are dead. *La tuberculose.*"

"Both of them? How ghastly! I'm sorry." The phrases tinkled emptily in the still air.

"*C'est comme ça,*" said Meknassy stonily. "My brother was *goumier.* He fight in Tunis and Italy, with the French. The Americans too. Much good it do him."

Cecilia ignored this thrust. "And what about your wife?"

If he found her rapid transitions impertinent, he didn't show it: "I have no more wife. Finished. We break the card."

"Break the card?"

"She give me no children, and then we go to the *cadi* and tear up the papers. You Americans do this too. Frenchmen not so often."

"You mean you're divorced?"

"*Divorcer,* that's it." He seized on this parallel with a tiger smile.

From his bower under the fig tree, the Frenchman watched uneasily. By all his lights, her conduct was evidently outrageous. When they had been assigned to Morocco two years earlier, Titus, method-

ical as always, had "indoctrinated" her: one couldn't meet the
Arabs on common ground. Another race, another religion—one
couldn't leap the barrier without upsetting the French, on whose
good will the new airbases would depend for—well, for everything.
And here she was, kicking over all the taboos. The foreman's hy-
pothesis was clear enough from his grin: lonely wives—nothing's too
low, not even an *indigène.*

But his presence only fueled Cecilia's recklessness. She sat down
on the steps and smoked and watched and listened, while Meknassy
alternated bursts of talk with the silent pouring of cement. Following the modulations of his asymmetrical face, now fired with emo-
tion, now fading into depths of indifference, she forced her eyes
away from the articulations of the shoulders and veined arms that
gleamed through the torn shirt. But as often as she looked away, she
looked back again.

"It is not good the Americans come always with the French," he
told her. "They make you treat the Moroccans just like they do."

"We can't come any other way, can we?"

"Plenty trouble for the *Fransoozi* soon, soon. For the Americans
too."

"And when both of us go, what will life be like?"

"It will be our own." His eyes flamed out at her. "What good you
ever bring to us?"

Through the gap in the wall behind him, Cecilia could see the
towers of the city and the jetties, like great arms embracing the distant blue. But that answer would be too easy. "All these things take
time," she said vaguely.

"Time, always time! There is not so much time as you think
—you and your friends." He brandished his trowel like a wea-
pon. But the gesture didn't carry: it was only undignified mimicry,
borrowed from the same source as his dictum on building from the
ground up. "We have other friends," he cried, "and better."

"And that life of your own—do you think it would last very long
with the friends you're talking about?"

"They cannot be worse than the *Fransoozi.*" He shrugged. "But
how can a woman—and a stranger—how can she understand?"

Cecilia's mouth went dry, but she managed a smile at the misogyny of Islam. "What is it exactly that we poor, weak-minded women can't understand?"

Meknassy didn't see that she was making fun of him. "Many things," he said. "Yes, many things. Let us begin with the police. Do the police beat you, madame, and then tell you that is something they give you to remember for a while?"

"And do the Americans beat you?"

"They leave that to the others. You are all the same, you *roumi:* you are all afraid. Of the Moroccans and the Algerians, and now of the Koreans—of all of us. Everywhere you work against us. But it is no matter. There will be another war. Maybe soon, maybe later— who knows? But this time it will be different: everything will come back against you."

"And not against you, I suppose." Her voice broke; the Frenchman looked around.

But Meknassy was immune to irony; his inoculation had killed the last microbes of doubt. "Each little thing," he went on ritually, wagging his head. "Everything will be repaid. A hundred times over."

And then as he raised his trowel again, she made out, under the tattered shirt, a thin, jagged scar that crossed the tawny back like lightning, from shoulder to waist. Meknassy's eye caught her glance.

"There are some things nobody can repair." He gave her a flash of gold teeth. "Not like your wall."

"Not like my wall," Cecilia echoed.

As she turned away, she found herself trembling on the edge of laughter.

4

Hot and exhausted, she dragged herself upstairs to dress for a dinner that the *Controleur Civil* of Casablanca was giving for the ranking Americans. She bathed in cold water, and when she had powdered herself, she stood for a minute before the long mirror in her dressing room. Cecilia had never shrunk from appraising the onset of her own autumn; tonight she found, as she drew herself up straight, that her body was weathering the decline better than her face. If only the line from shoulder to hip weren't broken by those puffy shadows at the waist—

Then she remembered the Moroccan's stare, and the wiry hand on her wrist. She covered her breasts with her hands. "We break the card," she said aloud. How old would *that* woman be? Suddenly a scenario unrolled before her. She looked at her watch; it was almost six.

She dabbed on her makeup and brushed her hair. Ruffling through her closet, she found her most naked evening dress. She slipped it over her head, snatched up wrap and bag, and hurried down the stairs.

Behind the brass-hinged front door she waited in a sickness of excitement until she heard the crunch of feet on the gravel. Meknassy and the Frenchman rounded the corner of the house, flinging good-natured monosyllables at one another. They threw down the tools by the hedge, and when their footsteps moved off toward the truck, Cecilia tugged open the heavy door. Carrying her wrap over one bare arm, she walked slowly down the steps and crossed the driveway to her car. The truck stood a few feet behind, but she did not look back at all.

The two men fell silent. But as she opened the door of her car, the Frenchman laughed. Then they started the truck, revving it up loudly. It roared past her with a scuffling of gravel. The foreman was at the wheel; Meknassy sat bolt upright beside him, his hawk profile turned straight ahead toward the road. And then they were gone in a cloud of dust.

Cecilia sat in her car for some time without moving. From the Arab shacks beyond the wall, the shrill melancholy of a reed flute drifted up on the evening air. In spite of the heat, she was shivering.

5

Next day she awoke late—it was almost noon—from a confusion of dreams. As an army wife, she was accustomed to nightmares, filled with circling danger. But this time it was not Titus who had been threatened. She recalled a wall of clouds; while she groped her way through it, a procession of tractors and jeeps and hybrid juggernauts like bulldozers had whizzed past, with the Colonel in the driver's seat of each, in full-dress uniform. She screamed up at him, but he looked neither right nor left. When she awoke, she was still giggling horribly.

At the *Controleur's* dinner she had drunk too much champagne. The wine, like everything else in Morocco, had operated freakishly. She had discovered in herself an inexhaustible vein of sarcasm: she had even stirred laughter at the expense of Jake Copps and his polyglot manpower pool.

"You certainly haven't persuaded our Meknassy," she said, "that he's getting much benefit from any of us—or from our valiant defense of the free world. It makes one wonder whether the Protectorate may not need a protector."

This was overheard by French officers; it did not go down well, and Jake Copps had been embarrassed.

Even after two cups of Manuela's blackest coffee, the images of her dreams hung before her. And as she climbed out of bed, her head throbbing faintly, she heard from the garden the clinking and slapping of a trowel.

It was the servants' afternoon off. When Cecilia had dismissed Manuela and the houseboy, she made up her mind to turn out a long letter for Titus. Thursday was her day for writing (the Colonel did not approve of irregular bursts of notes), and the house was quiet. If she could get the annoyances of the week down on paper, she might be able to turn her mind to something else.

For nearly an hour she sat at her desk, pecking about for bright bits of malice (other army wives often exclaimed over her amusing style) to deck out her narrative. The slap-slap of the trowel was hypnotic; when it stopped, she could barely resist peering through the shutters. But she steeled herself and picked up her pen again.

"We're indebted," she wrote, "to dear Jake Copps (who certainly hasn't forgotten that you and he are both due for promotion) for a Moroccan from Meknès, who has appeared on the scene, complete with tools and a French watchdog, to repair our ailing garden wall. I

hope his work will turn out sounder than his politics, which consist
of nationalism mixed up with weird versions of the Party
Line. . . . "

Then she foresaw the consequences of her flippancy. The Colonel
had purposes beyond his own prerogatives: he would never let her
chatter pass unnoticed, and if she maintained that last bit, there
would be a sequel for Meknassy. Did she want that?

Her eyes moved, as though on wires, to the picture on the big
table. The silver frame had stood there so long, among the leather
and brass of colonial loot, she had looked so often at the stolid pro-
consular lines of her husband's face, that the photograph had
become nothing more than a familiar ornament. Her memory kept
dredging up details that she wanted right now to forget: the tufts of
white hair on Titus's shoulder blades; his trick of licking his lips and
rolling up his eyes whenever he was about to interrupt her.

She picked her letter off the writing pad, tore it in half, and
dropped it into the wastebasket.

Just then there were three sharp knocks on the garden door. She
called for Manuela. But then she remembered: today there would be
no answer. She got up and went to the door.

For a second she hardly recognized the Moroccan. He had put on
his fez and his long gray djellaba, which was stained under the arms
with great hoops of sweat. Through the leaves of the fig tree behind
him, she could see the towered thunderheads gathering in the blue.

"What is it?" She opened the door a little wider.

He made her a sweeping bow; with his djellaba he had donned the
lordly manners of the Atlas. "Dare I to ask the gracious lady for a
glass of water?"

"Of course." She threw open the door (now she would show him
American manners), and he glided after her, his slippers shuffling
over the tiles. In the center of the kitchen he stood like a captive
animal, his eyes flashing over the rows of cupboards and shiny
fixtures. The sight of the table by the window, set for a solitary meal,
seemed to restore his confidence.

"You are much alone here?"

"Oh, I'm used to it. In the army, you know—But my husband is
not always away. Nor my sons."

She poured the water for him. *"Saha,"* he said. *"Barak allah houfik."* The goblet in his hand looked as fragile as Venetian glass.

"But what about the Frenchman?"

"He do not mind. I have earned my rest." Meknassy passed his hand expansively over his chest. "I am not a prisoner, madame."

Cecilia blushed. "You don't understand. I thought he might want water too."

"Oh, he is not thirsty, the *Fransoozi.*" He gave her the feline grin that meant a joke was afoot. "It is me who do the work, you know."

Cecilia forced a little laugh. "So it is. I suppose you're nearly finished."

"The work is done," he announced, with a kind of sly grandeur. "All done. Your wall is fine; it hold up good."

"I'm sure it will." She couldn't resist adding, "You built from the ground up, remember?"

Another tiger flash, this time a bit tremulous. "You are no longer angry then?"

"Why should I be angry? You are the mason, not I."

The conversation had reached a dead end, but he made no move to go. And Cecilia hung back from dismissing him as she should. He had become almost friendly, and rather helpless. Perhaps he regretted his own rancors. Perhaps he had forgiven her provocations.

"If I can be of any help to you," she said, "I'll be glad to send a note to Major Copps."

"A note?"

"To tell him how hard you worked—what a good job you did."

She squirmed at her own condescension, but Meknassy hardly noticed. "You haven't even seen the wall."

"There will be plenty of time for that. But I'm sure it's perfect. I'm really very grateful to you."

And Cecilia held out her hand.

The Moroccan hesitated, and when he raised his eyes to hers, she saw, at the corners of his embittered mouth, something that trembled on the edge of fear. Then it came over her what he must think, what he was leading up to. Or had she known it all along? Known it, and hoped for it?

She lowered her outstretched arm—it tingled as if asleep—and turned quickly away, but not quickly enough. The Moroccan stepped between her and the door and flung his arm around her neck. His fingers clawed into her shoulders, his long legs pressed hard against hers. And then she felt his open mouth on her neck and face, blindly searching for her lips; and the smell of his sweat filled the inner galleries of her nostrils.

For a minute she closed her eyes. She had a lightning vision of the scar across his back, and a warmth that was almost a tenderness rose in her. But before it engulfed her, she wrenched herself free. She fell away from him, and her hands grasped the cold porcelain of the sink behind her. "You had better go right away." She spoke as quietly as she could against the singing of blood in her ears. "You had better leave as fast as you can."

His astonishment gave her a flicker of pleasure: women were not all as simple as he thought.

"Why you send the cook and boy away?"

"I didn't send them away."

"I see them go."

"They always go on Thursday." She stifled her hysteria. "And what about the Frenchman? I would only have to call him, I could call him right now. But I won't. I won't say anything if you'll just go."

"Ah," said Meknassy, his face lighting with his recovered guile, "but when you call, the Frenchman not come."

"What have you done with him?"

"I do nothing. You do everything. All the week—and then last night. The *Fransoozi* is no friend, but he understand me." He crossed his arms. "And both of us—we understand you even better, madame."

His words sickened her more than his embrace. "You are crazy," she said, "crazy—both of you." But she knew this wasn't true. The signs and countersigns—the wink, the cupped hand—with which they had gauged the prospects transcended any national hatred. And she had answered—in another language perhaps, but she had answered.

"We are not crazy," Meknassy cried in his shallow voice. "You are a woman still, and no different from others."

So there she was: an experiment, a precedent—and no doubt hideously ancient. *"Va-t'en, va-t'en,"* She couldn't raise her voice above a nightmare whisper. "Get out. This minute."

And then at last he turned to go. She saw that he was weeping, his face twisted with rage, like a thwarted child. She heard the stamp of his *babouches* on the tiles and the banging of the shutters. From the window she watched for the last time, the sweep of his long legs under the djellaba as he rounded the corner of the house.

In the truck the Frenchman crouched over the wheel, his helmet pulled over his eyes, like a taxi-driver waiting for his client at a whorehouse.

When the crunching of tires on the gravel had died away, Cecilia stumbled out onto the terrace and down the garden steps. She watched the dusk spreading like a slow stain over the distant sea, and the blue-black thunderheads mounting, mounting in the south. Soon they would topple and there would be a storm—the first of the autumn—and an end to the heat.

The wall, as Meknassy had promised, was completely restored. A broad vein of white, untouched as yet by smut or moss, thrust its way up into the discolored concrete, with neat mortises to hold it firm. The Colonel would be well pleased.

But for her? "Each little thing," she said aloud. Under the wall's livid surface, her own eyes would never fail to catch the traces, faint but unmistakable, of something unrepaired and quite incapable of repair.

The Tigers of Wrath

None of Isaiah Ross's students went unmotivated for more than thirty seconds.

"He scared us pissless," was the way one young alumnus of Barton Country Day put it to me. "He even frightened me into learning the subjunctive of indirect discourse." His tone was reproachful, as though Mr. Ross were still alive and brandishing his pointer at him every morning.

I told him, a little condescendingly, that twenty years earlier than he, I had had a similar experience with verb prefixes that required the dative. "*Ad, ante, con, in, inter, ob . . .*" I began.

He gave me a haggard look. "*Post, prae, pro, sub,* and *super,*" he said, "and sometimes . . . sometimes . . . "

"And sometimes *circum,*" I completed tremulously.

But neither of us could explain what it was we had feared. There was the little green book, with its ink-fuzzed squares, in which Isaiah Ross, with a flourish of his double-ended pencil, marked one's "merits" (blue) or one's "demerits" (red). Looming at the end of every academic vista, there were the College Board Examinations and the possibility—appalling in the pre-dropout era—of failure and ejection into uncollegian outer darkness. But normally Mr. Ross (even across the gulf of half a century, I can't quite bring myself to call him Isaiah *tout court*) did not stoop to invoke the sanctions of the commonplace world that lay outside his classroom.

No, it was something else, impalpable but terribly real, that welled up into his every gesture: a certain frown that wrinkled his high, balding forehead when one jumped a caesura; a long-suffering glance at Ingres's "Reading from Homer," which hung above the blackboard, as he waited with mock patience for an answer; an agitated ruffling of his pompadour if one misconstrued a gerundive. And then there was the long pointer, with its white rubber tip, the scepter of excommunication and the staff of support, bending perilously in moments of pedagogic frustration. The fledglings who trembled at their one-armed desks in Room 21 could hardly be expected to understand that they were in the presence of the Platonic Ideal; but they knew that failure, however minor, was shameful.

Looking back over the decades that narrow away in my inverted telescope, I find it miraculous that one man could have deployed for nearly fifty years an unflagging enthusiasm in the defense and illumination of a language that fluctuated so wildly in the academic scale of values. Nothing could shake his confidence in the efficacy of Horace and Virgil for the polishing of crude minds; and he remained faithful to Baker and Inglis's *Latin Composition* (I still see that beige cover with its menacing block print) as the prime therapy for sagging syntax. Apparently he left as deep a mark on the languid cynics of the 1950s as he did on innocents such as I, who sat under him—I use the phrase advisedly, for I see now that he was in every sense a *grand maître*—during the coming of age that followed the First World War. Roman *Virtus* carried him through fourteen years of retirement, and when he died in 1968 at the age of eighty-one, a chorus of alumni joined in recognizing him as one of the last American practitioners of the classic prep-school disciplines.

Quite unexpectedly my own memoir, published in the school magazine, evoked a letter from Mr. Ross's younger brother (he was seventy-eight), in which he fixed the beginning of Isaiah's career at the dawn of the century. At the age of twelve, in the kitchen of a New Hampshire farmhouse, he had astonished his parents and brothers one morning by diagramming on the side of the black iron stove an overpowering sentence from Gibbon. "Isaiah showed us that every part of that sentence—it was something about the Empress Theodora—fitted exactly with some other part. He had discovered that Gibbon's syntax, like that of Cicero, was jointed like a Roman aqueduct. And he wouldn't let us go until we had shared his excite-

ment. I guess at that moment he decided that teaching was the real
right thing. And as you know, nothing but the best would ever do; he
didn't need to raise his voice to make you sure of that."

"Nothing but the best." Mr. Ross's brother was right. And naturally he had no way of knowing that on one occasion, Isaiah, under
the stress of dyspepsia, did raise his voice. His isolated outburst gave
me my only glimpse into the depths of his soul; it haunts me to this
day, like Henry James's nightmare flight through the Galerie
d'Apollon. And it had the same effect on me: it awoke me to the
reality of the past. Odd that the duodenal ulcer of an obscure Latin
master should have brought a gangling adolescent to a great di-
vide—but there it was. In the tame and even tenor of the Barton
School, one felt that the earth had trembled.

2

The rise of the Barton Country Day School ("Cares for the boy all
day") belongs to the same era as the advent of Isaiah Ross, although
at this distance he seems to me the more venerable of the two. In
1915 the first families of Minneapolis—the princes of flour milling
and lumberyards and farm mortgages; the earls of Lake Superior,
who ravaged the subsoil unchecked, in their search for iron ore—
decided that without severing the umbilical cord as the British did,
they wanted their sons and daughters to have a decent preparation
for the ultimate pilgrimage to the universities of the Ivy League. The
egalitarianism of pioneer days had faded into the snobbery of the
second generation: our parents were convinced that a schoolmaster
from Yale or a schoolmistress from Vassar could set a better tone
than the harried and underpaid worthies of the public schools. They
were attracted also by the concept of the country day school: here
was a chance to remove their children from the contamination (as
they saw it) of the city high schools, with their unbuttoned curricula
and their promiscuous hurly-burly. (There was the standard joke
about the old maid who had discovered that at public schools boys
and girls actually *matriculated* together.)

As the circle of affluence widened, the school stirred and put forth new shoots. The curriculum grew to include the full twelve years of secondary education. Dr. Barton, a gentle and slightly weary scholar, retired to Boston; he was succeeded by a more "go-getting" headmaster, Dr. Elson, a brisk problem-solver from Yale, irreproachably low-church and adept at buttering up the trustees and extorting memorial windows. The upper grades (or "rooms," as our parents persisted in calling them) moved from a modest shingled house on Pleasant Avenue to a crenellated pink brick castle of vaguely Tudor inspiration twelve miles beyond the city limits.

Barton was generously endowed. Its tone, like that of its feminine counterpart, the Collegiate School (in the co-educational rage of the sixties the two schools merged), remained "exclusive." Even in the Great Depression, trustees and faculty were unabashedly elitist—"persnickety" was my father's phrase—in sorting out the hopefuls who applied for admission. As late as 1932, the sixteen members of my class who stepped forward in rented caps and gowns to receive their sheepskins were nearly all WASPs of impeccable antecedents. As hostages to progressivism, there were two Catholics, one Jew, and one "Scandahoovian" Lutheran. Only one of the Catholics was Irish, and his Hibernian taint was mitigated not by lace curtains but by athletic glory: "Fizzy" Fitzgerald was a hockey champion of statewide renown. There were no black students and no applicants. "Nor like to be," my Uncle George, a senior trustee, told me firmly. He and Dr. Elson considered that the four exotics already constituted a daring dosage.

The atmosphere of the final quadrennium at Barton is consecrated in the school anthem. This was the joint production of Lincoln Talcott of the English Department, another senior luminary, and young Donald Laser, who taught European history with an anti-European bias, played the chapel organ and dazzled the secretaries in Dr. Elson's office with his pencil-line mustache:

> High above the rolling country, far from noise and smoke,
> Strong and clean her noble towers in their wood of oak.
> Barton, Barton, sing her praises, keep her honor bright;
> Pass the torch to those that follow with an undimmed light.

As a graduate of Cornell, Isaiah Ross lost no time in pointing out that the collaborators had plagiarized "Cayuga's Waters"—perceptibly in the lyric, grossly in the music.

"And your syntax," he told Mr. Talcott gleefully, "is wobbly. That undimmed light—are we passing it or following with it? In Latin you have to be more careful when you play around with hysteron proteron."

These strictures touched off a dispute that smoldered for years: English and History lined up against Latin and Romance Languages (which in fact consisted entirely of French). There Isaiah found a backer in Edouard Bosanquet ("Bosco"), another perfectionist, who had come to Minnesota through chance contacts in the Lafayette Escadrille. Bosco wore a walrus mustache as unkempt as Laser's was slick, and he suspected his colleague, quite justly, of poisoning young minds against the Bourbon monarchy. In general, he nourished a faint contempt for Anglo-Saxon sentimentalism. "'Strong and clean'—*qu'est-ce que ça fait que les tours soient propres?"* he once asked me rhetorically. *"Moi, je préfère le bruit et la fumée, vous savez."*

What neither authors nor detractors seemed to realize was that the anthem, like the school itself, was a hangover from the universe of Tennyson. That rolling country, those bright torches, the clean towers that Bosco found so objectionable—unquestionably they came from *chez Alfred*. And the exhortation could have dropped as naturally from the lips of Rugby's Doctor Arnold as from the fountain pen of Mr. Talcott.

The interior of our castle, although highly functional and comfortably heated, also bore traces of Victorian medievalism. There were pointed arches in the gymnasium and mullioned windows in the refectory. The walls of the library were covered with Arthurian frescoes in the style of Puvis de Chavannes. The classrooms contained the regulation portraits of Shakespeare and Wordsworth and Hawthorne in their most respectable and sheep-like phases; but they were overshadowed by gigantic sepia reproductions of Edwin Austin Abbey in ponderous frames: knights of the grail, or vigil-keeping squires who belonged to the prep-school "age group." In those noble towers, with their smell of soap and floor wax, there was no place for Guinevere or the Lady of Shalott.

Faithfully every morning, in autumn haze or flying snow, we sons of Barton, clutching at disordered books and papers (briefcases were bad form) and wiping the egg smears from our lips, embarked in the long yellow trolleys of the Twin City Rapid Transit. Wearily every evening, we reembarked for the city, our muscles aching from the exertions of field and diamond, our stomachs filled with hot cocoa and saltines, our heads spinning with quadratic equations and the laws of Newton (how could we know they had already been repealed by a wild-haired German who would presently appear at Princeton?), our pulses quickened by the campaigns of the Civil War, the rough-and-tumble of Shakespeare and Molière, and— transcendent for me—the grandeur of Virgil, glimpsed in flashes through the rhetorical clouds that floated around the brow of Isaiah Ross.

3

Years later, when my turn came to visit the school as an outlander from New England, I was surprised to learn from Edouard Bosanquet that Isaiah's debut at Barton had not been auspicious.

"By the time you were a senior," Bosco explained, "it was quite different. He could hold himself in reserve for the Horatian and Virgilian phases and leave the underlings to prepare the ground. He was like an archbishop in a parish church, where the lower clergy are expected to surrender the chalice at the big moments."

"I don't see Dr. Elson surrendering any chalices."

"Elson was no good at languages, so in the end he had to yield too. But in the beginning he resisted. He talked a lot about the lost digamma and kept Isaiah busy with Caesar, where he couldn't deploy his *mystique*. And Isaiah was painfully shy."

"'Isaiah Ross was shy?"

"Oh, in his *for interieur* he had all the confidence in the world. But, as we say in France, he did not exteriorize himself very well. At least not in the beginning."

Bosco then told me, with a chuckle, that initially Isaiah had been intimidated by Dr. Elson's white mane and tweedy elegance and by the flossy manners of his wife. Thinking to expose the newcomer to the best traditions of Minneapolis, Mrs. Elson telephoned to ask him to Thanksgiving dinner. But the overture miscarried.

"I am already engaged," Isaiah told her shrilly. At moments of distress his voice always ascended several registers.

Mrs. Elson murmered soothingly that he must make it another time; she would call him again.

But the suavity of Horace was no match for Isaiah's panic before the omnivorous hospitality of the Midwest. "I'm afraid the situation is the same for Christmas," he said. There was a pause. "And that goes for New Year's too," he added.

Isaiah Ross never married. He conducted flirtations, closely watched by students and faculty, with opposite numbers on the staff of the Collegiate School. Unlike Don Laser, whose Ford had been seen parked near haunts of vice on La Salle Avenue, Isaiah was no candidate for debauchery. He would have cut an incongruous figure in Minneapolis speakeasies, where the wine was anything but Falernian. And the ladies of Collegiate were as spinsterly and perfectionist as he.

In my time, Isaiah shared an apartment with another bachelor, the town's leading distributor of hearing aids. The roommate's forte was cooking rather than classics, and their cohabitation caused discreet smiles among our elders. In those days bedroom doors were kept firmly shut, and I see no point in consigning Isaiah to any special niche among consenting adults. The awe, and finally the affection, with which his students regarded him was untainted by any *arrière-pensée* that I recall. We found him formidable in class. We were even impressed on the tennis court; with long practice, he had developed a serve known as the "Ross tornado"—a terrific wind-up, with one foot pawing the air momentarily, like a charger, and then an all-out smash that put the ball just where white powder would fly from the forward line. And basically, his attitude toward us was like that of Lyautey toward the Moroccans: "He burned to be of service." If he added to his mission the same "*parcelle d'amour*" that the Marshal reserved for his, it would be gratuitous to attach a clinical label to it.

4

My own encounter with what Bosco called Isaiah's *for interieur* arose, as I have said, from a digestive aberration. In my senior year, Mr. Ross suffered from an incipient ulcer. As Virgil (which, unlike the other Latin poets, was a College Board subject and therefore compulsory) came just before lunch, Isaiah used to burp, discreetly but not inaudibly, as he unrolled the soft and solemn hexameters of the *Aeneid*. In addition to making him rather cross with the less adept catechumens, his affliction introduced startling variations into the prosody of Virgil: it lent unexpected realism to the caprices of Aeolus, God of the Winds; it livened up the woebegone greetings of Dido:

"*Haud ignara*—oop—*mali, miseris succerrere*—oop—*disco.*"

In the sterner passages these gastric caesurae were admittedly less felicitous:

"*Timeo Danaos*—oop—*et dona ferentes.*"

With the timeless cruelty of youth, we used to pencil the score on the edges of our desks, sitting bolt upright as we strained our ears for the next innovative burst. Had we been old enough to realize the misery that caused Mr. Ross's unaccustomed sharpness, we might have been less obsessed with the sorrows that accrued to our weaker Latinists. But in the end his sarcasms produced a Gladiators' Revolt.

The *bête noire*—but he was not alone—was Fizzy Fitzgerald, the blue-eyed alien I have mentioned already. Fizzy's prowess on the hockey rink did not carry over into the arena of Latin. He might shoot a hundred goals during the winter, but Isaiah Ross was not disarmed so long as he failed to distinguish the ablative of agency from the ablative of specification. On his side, Fizzy resented his humiliation at the hands of the Protestants; it was not his own choice, after all, that had brought him to suffer *in partibus infidelium*. His golden hair and Irish charm and the aura of athletic heroism did the rest: we all agreed that Papists and Protestants should join for once in defense of fair play.

At first we tried, like small birds besieged by a hawk, to organize a community defense. On the outgoing trolley car, knots of collaborators would cluster around me for guidance: I may have been a bust on the baseball diamond, but my supremacy in exegesis was unquestionable. Together we would go over the texts of the day and prepare what was in effect a collective crib. While this enhanced the performance of the strong, it did little to protect the weak. Mr. Ross's practiced ear quickly tuned in on false quantities: unerringly he picked out the feebler of the flock, for whom he reserved the toughest morsels. And then he would swoop down in wrath, like Juno tormenting her rivals. Once again, Fizzy and the others would flutter and flounder in the outbursts of his scorn.

Finally I was chosen—unwisely as it turned out—to serve as spokesman for a Grand Remonstrance. The responsibility appalled me; still I rather relished my transformation from a mousy dean of Latinists into a hefty Spartacus, who would bring justice to the helots of Barton Country Day. At sixteen I was a promising student but more than a shade priggish; like Clarence Day, I was credulous to the point where I might just as well have been stupid. My inexperience couldn't foresee the reaction of Isaiah Ross: all I anticipated was anger, but anger followed by repentance.

So I bided my time in dread, waiting for clear-cut aggression that would justify my *démarche*. It wasn't long in coming: despite careful coaching, Fizzy stumbled one morning over the passive periphrastic and fell flat.

"*Monstrum horrendum*," said Isaiah in the clipped accents of despair, "is not 'enormous horror' for heaven's sake! Now tell us, Fitzgerald, what part of speech is *monstrum?*"

"Noun, I guess," said Fizzy sullenly.

"You guess right. And what is *horrendum*, please?"

Fizzy's glance flickered desperately in my direction. I could only clench my hands under my book and pray. "Genitive, I guess," he faltered.

"Genitive, you guess!" cried Isaiah. "My dear sir, you guessed wrong. It's a gerundive, a gerundive. 'A monster *to be* feared.'" He turned wearily toward the rest of us. "What is the construction, gentlemen?" (Isaiah Ross always called us "gentlemen," never "boys" or "fellows" like Dr. Elson.)

I maintained the silence of solidarity, but the traitor behind me blurted out "passive periphrastic." This was greeted by subdued groans.

"The passive periphrastic," said Isaiah in mock sorrow. "Our old, old friend. And you passed him right by. Don't you remember '*delenda est Carthago*'?"

"No, sir," said Fizzy.

Mr. Ross braced his hands behind him against the trough of the blackboard, in which he had carefully deposited the pointer. His brow wrinkled like the brow of Laocoön. "I think Virgil is not your specialty."

"Oh no, sir," panted Fizzy, his cheeks flaming.

"Nor Latin. Nor grammar. Nor poetry. '*De gustibus non est disputandum.*'"

"Sir?"

"Another periphrastic. But I won't translate. Any hockey star should understand that one. Your classmates will be glad to explain."

There was a sharp, collective intake of breath. My hour had come, my duty was clear.

When the bell rang, I stayed in my seat. The others filed out, glancing back at me in pity and terror, but not without Rochefoucauldian relish for my predicament. Mr. Ross looked at me curiously but not unkindly. I pulled up my socks (literally) and rose in my place.

"Sir," I began hoarsely, "we don't . . . we don't think it's fair."

"Fair? What do you mean? What isn't fair?"

"Well, to pick on Fizzy and the others."

"Pick on them?" His voice rose several keys. "I pick on nobody. I pick on mistakes, no matter who makes them."

"But for some of us it's always much tougher."

I still see myself standing there in my salt-and-pepper knicker-bockers and belted jacket, my fingers twisting, my bangs clinging damply to my forehead, my pink ears growing pinker. I really hadn't much to say, but my fear of consequences kept me babbling on, like one of Dostoevsky's compulsive buffoons. At length my allocution—the memory of it makes my toes curl—trailed off in a plea for indulgence and restraint. "If only you'd be more careful, sir, how you talk to Fizzy," I implored.

Mr. Ross raked at his pompadour for several seconds. "Had you really expected," he said softly, "that I would let blunders of that sort pass in my classes? That I wouldn't say a word?"

I said I didn't think the passive periphrastic was all that important.

"Mistakes have to be corrected," he told me, "and with a knife sometimes, not a smile. That's what teachers are for."

Clearly he was flabbergasted, but not in the way I had expected. Vexation with my impertinence had turned to distress at my weak-kneed humanitarianism. Knowing that I shared his passion for Virgil and that I had even responded to the urbanity of Catullus (he had lent me the *Odes* to try outside of class), he had come to nurture a certain tenderness for me. Perhaps at Harvard I would do credit to the school and to him. Perhaps something of the grandeur that was Rome would stick to my ribs for good. And now here I was, his prize acolyte, defending the duffers and telling him prissily to watch his language. Obviously, the infusion of Roman iron had proven too feeble.

The ball seemed to be in my court. "Maybe you could go a little easier on everyone," I ventured, pushing back my bangs. "Like in baseball. I'm lousy at baseball, but Jonesy—Mr. Jones—doesn't get sore at me. Not too sore anyway."

"Baseball!" said Isaiah, as though I had mentioned something faintly obscene. "And hockey! But that's not what we're talking about. Not at all."

"I know that, sir. It's just that I. . . . "

"No, no." Isaiah flapped his hands impatiently. "And I'm not sore at Fitzgerald personally. He's a fine boy. I'm sure it's not easy for him at Barton. And no one can touch him on the hockey rink. But in Latin class, he needs to hear me crack the whip."

Knives and whips! I must have looked shocked, because Isaiah added, with a smile, "I'm perhaps falling into catachresis. Let's say that Fitzgerald needs the referee's whistle. And so do the others. All of you really. Because if I were to let Fitzgerald's mistakes slip by, the rest of you wouldn't have any benchmarks either. Anyway," he said wickedly, "just think how the Jesuits would handle him."

Our conversation was taking directions undreamed of by my classmates. Or by me. I could see the rocks of disloyalty looming ahead. I wanted to cut and run. But I was becoming hypnotized. So I stood riveted to the floor of Room 21 while Isaiah Ross, who had recovered his balance—and with it, a certain afflatus—explained to me what the classics really meant.

Long after conjugations and declensions had faded from my memory and nothing but tag ends of poetry remained in my mental *impedimenta* (neuter plural, second), I was to hark back to that moment. I got then my first inkling that Latin carried with it an alluvium far more precious than the language itself: the sense of contact with eternal civic and martial virtues; the touchstones of Virgilian splendor, or Horatian amenity, that would condition all later judgments of poetry; the wonders of the mythological world, whose magic was already fading into exoticism; the mastery of a condensed and articulated syntax that made the intricacies of modern language (including one's own) pale into insignificance.

Am I sentimentalizing? Maybe. I know that many of my contemporaries fiercely reject dead languages; they see them as straitjackets rather than free-flowing tunics. And they are repelled by the bitter perfume of classical wisdom. All I can say is that Isaiah Ross managed to turn my eyes toward the span of an entire civilization, whose somber finale gave me in later days a vantage point: from there, as he told me, I could view and even project, however imperfectly, my own unfinished era.

"At least I hope it won't be finished," he wound up. "That depends on all of you. With Greece and Rome, it really *is* finished. We know the end of the story. It's all over—washed up, wiped out—and that's what makes it so useful for us. All of it." He burped softly and looked at his watch. "Even the passive periphrastic."

I stood for a minute, breathing a bit heavily, and then he stepped down from the desk platform. "Don't worry too much about your classmates' tender toes," he said. "They'll live. They'll live to do imitations of me." As we moved toward the door, he swiveled around toward me. "Do you know Blake at all? I don't suppose Lincoln Talcott has given you 'The Proverbs of Hell'?"

I shook my head.

" 'The tigers of wrath are wiser than the horses of instruction.' Remember that, the next time you think I'm getting tough. There's just one other thing."

"Yes, sir."

"Don't ever forget, my dear John, to save a little wrath for yourself."

At the sound of my first name, I blushed again. But with a difference: I was old enough to realize that I was being suborned and still young enough to enjoy it.

"We're late for lunch," Mr. Ross said crisply. At the door he grasped my elbow. "Tomorrow I want to talk to you about the elective for the second term. There will be only four of you. This year I think we might cut out the Ovid—I really find the *Metamorphoses* are rather old hat—and that will leave more time for Catullus. We might even try a bit of Lucretius"—he lowered his voice conspiratorially—"if Dr. Elson's religious principles will permit."

I told him that it sounded great.

5

In the refectory curious eyes turned toward the latecomers. Forks paused in mid-course as we took our places at the Senior table under the disapproving stare of Dr. Elson. Fizzy raised his golden eyebrows at me from across the crockery. I had a moment of panic, with butterflies in the stomach, as on the night of the school play.

"After lunch," I whispered, spearing a sausage from the platter.

I didn't eat much. My head whirled with visions of past and future, of duffers trailing clouds of glory, of novices to whom we must pass the undimmed light. I saw that my report to the class would have to be heavily censored. I had delivered the message; the days to come would tell the tale.

One awkward question: what if Mr. Ross remained unmoved by our protest? If his rampages broke out again, young Spartacus would be in a fine pickle with the other gladiators.

At the far end of the table, the president of the student council, who always sat on Isaiah's right, was angling for his attention. Isaiah nodded a little absently and then craned down to listen, the fingers of his left hand playing with bread crumbs on the shiny table. In his right hand, he held a large glass of milk, from which he took careful sips. Gradually the furrows cleared from his forehead; the domed brow was again serene.

At one moment he looked up, and his eyes met mine. He would never have permitted himself a wink; there wasn't even a ghost of a smile. But there had been a contact. The tigers of wrath were leashed. They weren't dead, though; and as they had ended by making us accomplices, I didn't think that either of us would let the other down.

The Lady of Shalott

"I am half sick of shadows," said
The Lady of Shalott.
—Tennyson

Twisting and turning through the passes in her rented Fiat, Victoria
scanned the lunar landscape of the Atlas Mountains for some trace
of the dimly remembered past. At last she sighted the white mass of
Fez, and then the minarets and ramparts, like battlements of
Camelot in the fading light. After several false leads (she had never
learned Arabic, and her French proved less adaptable than she had
hoped), she was relieved to turn a corner and run smack into the
Palais Jamai. The new order had spared the bogus Moorish
splendors of the hotel, but tiles had fallen from mosaics and letters
from signs. "Maintenance," Victoria said to herself, "upkeep: the
true secret of civilization." Another promising theme for an article.

But why did she have to alchemize everything she saw or heard
into captions on glossy paper? She longed suddenly for a touch of
warmth, of reality without reserve or calculation. Once installed in
the Jamai, she pushed aside the prospect of sunset snapshots from
the Merinide tombs, and after wrestling with the plumbing, she
managed a hot bath. For some time she sat fixing her hair, paying
special attention to thin spots.

David arrived from Casablanca in time for dinner. When Victoria
went down, he was standing impassively, hands folded in front of
him, in the dusky courtyard. She had time for a once-over before he
saw her. She didn't want to view anyone—least of all an ex-husband—

with a finicky eye, but she was rather taken aback. His blue serge suit (it wasn't one she remembered) was shiny and badly brushed even in the filtered light of the lanterns, and the points of his shirt collar curled slightly. His face was shiny too and darkened to mahogany by the same sun that had whitened his hair. He looked like a settler of thirty years ago, a modest *pied noir* in from the hills for a weekend of drinking and whoring in the Reserved Quarter. Victoria regretted her pleated pyjamas and pearls and painstaking makeup: travel-worn tweeds and flying hair would have done better, but without bringing her down quite to his level.

David's greeting was shy but casual: a peck on each cheek, as though he had left her at the editorial offices for a day rather than for five years on another continent. They ate at the hotel, stowing away couscous and sugared pigeon pie with hardly a word between them. Gradually Victoria's constraint evaporated: marital silences were a relief from the unassimilated chatter of press cocktails and the buzz-buzz of the Tangier international set. At last David pushed his plate away and took out his pipe, which, after a glance from her, he did not light.

"Would you like to wander about?" he asked. "I see your name all over the dear old magazine whenever I run onto a copy, so I suppose that Schroeder has sent you and Alice Johns out to put Morocco on the map."

She ignored his irony. "I never quite got to know Fez when I—when we were here before. But really, David, I came to see you. I've left Alice in Tangier."

"Ageless Alice! I see her slogging through the Casbah with the same gaggle of cameras around her neck."

"Exactly right! She'll polish off the hashish set and the international butterflies. Then I'll move in on artists and writers."

"You won't find many. Gone with the French. Morocco has gotten expensive and kind of shaky. There's almost no one left down my way."

"What about you? Don't tell me you're the only painter around."

"Me a painter?" his dark face stiffened. "I've melted into the landscape, that's all. But what about Fez? It'll take you back to the

Middle Ages. Unlike Tangier, it's authentic—something real for a journalist to get her teeth into."

"You never did take my work seriously, but then basically I guess I don't either."

He smiled. "Basically," he said with an edge of mockery, "I don't take anything very seriously nowadays. I put all the labels away when I left the magazine."

For "magazine" read "you," Victoria thought. But was he playing it straight? He had certainly changed: he had grown heavier—not fat exactly, but jowly and creased of neck—and powerful in a relaxed, Mediterranean way. That David took nothing seriously—not even his painting—she didn't believe for a minute. What was he hiding behind the beachcomber's mask?

Fez, as David had promised, was all of a piece, but Victoria wasn't sure she could stomach the coherence of Islam. For nearly an hour they picked their way through windowless canyons, opening above to deep blue and to stars exploding like rockets. They paused before lighted enclaves: *fondouks* crammed with copper vessels and piles of flashy cloth; little houses in the Reserved Quarter, where the women waited silently in tiled doorways. Now and then a mule tinkled past on feet as soundless as those of the slippered, white-robed men who flitted by like ghosts. David kept pulling her up short by the elbow to avoid refuse in their path or leprous figures that darted out of the shadows, whining, with outstretched hands. He dismissed them with a grunt, and Victoria took his arm in the guise of camaraderie but also with secret relief.

And yet her relief was suffused with a desire for something she couldn't define. Everywhere she caught the sweetish aroma of cooking oil and spice and ordure that shakes the heart of the North African traveler with the momentary excitement of carnality and death among strangers.

After a time David complained that his shoes pinched (Victoria smiled at the thought that he might be used to going barefoot), and they sank down on a bench outside the Karouiine Mosque, from which came the plash of a hidden fountain and a soft ululation.

"Tell me, David, what do you do with yourself down here?"

"Oh, lots of things but nothing much." He folded his hands over one knee. She could see how work had coarsened them. "I raise tomatoes and artichokes. I breed hunting dogs. I've bought a truck to haul sand into Casablanca for buildings. The Moroccans are still putting up schools and cheap flats. I've got a beat-up station wagon; Abdul—that's my driver—picks up a few pennies for me, driving villagers to the souks. There's bathing—a great beach—and a lot of surf-fishing. And that's about it."

That was it! He offered no handle, no rough edge, for her to get hold of. But the bleakness struck her as artificial: if he didn't talk about his real work, there must be a reason. Perhaps his detachment concealed his old awe for Victoria, the arbiter of taste. He may even have feared a gibe: she remembered, with regret, that when he had announced five years ago that he was leaving her—it was right after the magazine had sent them on a smart-set mission to Marrakesh— she had made a cutting reference to Gauguin.

"It all sounds very peaceful, your new life," she said. "Don't you hanker for a change now and then? No plans or projects?"

"No one makes plans in Morocco any more—except the King maybe, and his mostly go haywire. So we all drift. But you should come down and have a look." His irony gave way to a muffled urgency, a childlike insistence. "I'm sure you'd like the house."

"I'm sure I would. It's kind of a long way, though, just to look at a house."

He flipped his hand. "It's the whole set-up you ought to see. You'll get some idea of Moroccan life in this year of our Lord—and in the glorious era of Independence. If you get bored, there's always Casa or your beloved Marrakesh." He got up, but she didn't move; once again he had ducked her. "Besides," he added, a shade embarrassed, "I could use a lift. I couldn't take my wagon off the road on market day, so I left it with Abdul and hitched a ride with one of the Fassi in a truck."

"For God's sake, David, you shouldn't have come all that way. That was sweet of you." She looked away. "Could you really put me up?"

"Not in the style you're used to, but, as you say, it's peaceful. It would do you good, Victoria."

"Peace!" She flicked the dust from her shoes with her scarf and got up. "If I ever sit down long enough to think, it will probably be the end of me."

But after tossing and turning most of the night (David had not laid siege to her room as she had half expected), she sent a telegram to Alice Johns: "Need more time for South. Hope you can swing Tangier. *Poste-restante Ain-el-Ma près Casablanca.*" That would keep everybody guessing—not excluding herself. Any why not? The magazine owed her something more than a living. She might return for once with something longer-lived than a chichi travelogue.

In front of the house, a sandbank, covered with dune grass, dropped to a wide beach and to the crash and green swirl of the Atlantic, where Arabs and their naked children bathed and fished. At the back, grass huts clustered around a tiny whitewashed shrine with a dome. The fellahs in their colored rags moved up and down the rows of tomato vines, hoeing the reddish soil or carrying water in earthen jars. Pigtailed children tagged at their heels or played among the cactuses. After the rains, David told Victoria, the brown fields beyond the Casablanca road would be green-gold with waving barley, and dotted almost overnight with the crimson of wild poppies.

"Sounds lovely," Victoria said. "Remember the view in the Lady of Shalott's mirror?"

"It's a lot like that, come to think of it." He squinted mischievously. "But you remember what happened to her."

"She left her mirror, didn't she, to get a straight look at Lancelot."

"And whammo! The mirror cracked right down the middle."

"Whammo is right. But she did get the eye from Lancelot."

"Too late, though; she never knew what hit her."

The house was a rambling improvisation of dark beams and blazing white plaster. All of it was on one floor, mostly a big living room strewn with poufs and rope-backed chairs and coarse wool rugs. At the back were two flimsily partitioned sleeping spaces with washstands (Victoria accepted her accessibility—and David's—with an unconcern that covered a throb of anticipation). At the side was a lean-to kitchen with a kerosene stove. Toilet and shower were outside; the bathtub was the ocean. David's dogs slunk in and out of the house, sniffing about the low tables, laying their huge, mournful heads in her lap.

In all the rooms she caught the faint, fleshy smell that had agitated her in Fez.

"Standard everywhere," David said curtly. "Oil and herbs and assorted crap. The perfume of Islam. You'll get used to it."

"You talk as if I were settling in."

He flushed. "That'll be the day!"

Besides the driver, David kept one servant, a *fatma* named Hadouch, who came across from the grass huts in the morning with her little boy. More neatly dressed than the women one met along the road, and unveiled, she had evidently been exempted from work in the fields. She had a strong-jawed brown face, lightly tattooed about the chin, and clear gray eyes. Even the baggy trousers and voluminous *haik* could not conceal that Hadouch had lost her figure. But she had kept a fine carriage, as though perpetually balancing a water jar on her head. Every morning she stared blankly at Victoria; she might have been seeing her for the first time. Then she touched her lips and her breast, with her fingers fanned out, and dropped a silent curtsey. Was she invoking a spell, Victoria wondered, or warding one off?

The boy Mehdi followed his mother everywhere—a handsome, erect child of about four, with lighter skin and stolid hazel eyes. More Berber than Arab, Victoria surmised. Under his miniature djellaba, with its embroidered hems, he wore blue jeans. His head was shaved, like those of the other children, except for the tiny pigtail.

"That's to draw him up to heaven," David explained. "It's the same idea as the tassel on the fez. Kids don't have an easy time down here. So one has to be prepared."

The glance he gave the boy was rather seignorial. Victoria stirred with an unaccustomed regret for her own childlessness.

In the recesses formed by the beams, David had hung his paintings. The larger canvases were conventional—Moroccans seen through western eyes: peasants, fishermen, notables in burnooses, women peeping from behind veils. The biggest was a nude, with her head thrown back into the shadow so as to highlight the dark, heavy breasts and swollen belly. A competent pastiche: Renoir clouded by Toulouse-Lautrec—nothing more. The forcible-feeble note strengthened Victoria's hope—unmitigated by her recognizing it as unworthy—that his separation from her had led to precious little.

But was that quite just? In the corners near the fireplace, he had stacked several smaller things, unframed. When she turned them to the light she saw that they were seascapes, or landscapes, but always with water in motion. Marine Cezanne? Winslow Homer? The composition verged on the abstract, but it was not static. Clearly David had evolved it on his own, and not without sweat. Victoria resolved to stop labeling and pigeonholing: perhaps it was she who was derivative.

When David came in with his casting rod, he found her holding a canvas at arm's length. He filled his pipe, watching her closely.

She allowed a suitable pause for inspection. "Tell me, have you been doing these things long?"

"Oh, I've made a lot of false starts. I'm not sure I've quite got it yet." He was very off-hand. "You think they're good?"

"I like them a lot. You should work more on that type of picture."

"I have to eat first. That takes work too."

But he sounded pleased, and she turned up the volume. "I mean it, David. Alice and I know people who are looking for fresh stuff. And Morocco's on the front page again—Islam and guerrillas and so on."

"I see: native arts and crafts from the tinderbox of North Africa?"

"Do you have to be so defensive? You might at least try them out on someone. Is what's-his-name Bernaud still in Casablanca?"

"If I start peddling my pictures instead of artichokes, I'll starve."

All this hesitation, she was sure, concealed a fear, and therefore a desire, perhaps the most insidious of all desires. She nosed up to it. "You don't need to peddle. Why not let me have a try?"

"I don't kid myself. But some of those things I rather like, even if nobody else does."

"I envy you. I make my living by pleasing everyone but myself."

"Maybe that's better."

His remoteness was maddening. "Don't you ever resent my success?"

"Why the hell should I, Victoria? Actually it makes me feel easier."

"Easier?"

"About our breaking up. At least one of us has made out all right."

She sighed and dropped into a chair. "No need for apologies. I wasn't exactly the ideal wife."

"Oh, it wasn't really you. It was everybody. It was New York and Paris and the magazine—all the sophisticated crap. It was everything. And I was no rose either."

Victoria found this exculpation more wounding than a hundred reproaches he might have made. Her humility had missed its mark.

After a minute he said, "No harm in your trying out the little pictures—that is, if you'd get a bang out of it. But why not try some of the bigger things too, the figures?"

"Why not?" Victoria smiled. "Yes, why not?"

More easily than she had reckoned, Victoria phased into the monotony of Moroccan autumn. While David was off with the truck, she rattled over the stony roads in the Fiat to fetch mail from the tiny post office (Alice and the others seemed to have dropped her into oblivion) or just to sit on the dunes. Once she went along in the station wagon for the circuit of the village markets. The seats were crammed with Arabs, and the roof covered with their sacks and battered baskets and live chickens. On the way home David stopped to sketch, while his passengers squatted stoically by the roadside with teapots and sugar loaves. A flash of silver teeth, and hands reached toward them with cups of mint tea; only David accepted. Victoria heard guttural imprecations against the sketches: the taboos of Islam, David explained; he didn't seem to mind.

Victoria took care not to hang over him, and he didn't raise a beckoning finger. Most of the day they were outdoors or under the eyes of Abdul or Hadouch. In the evening they smoked and yawned and exchanged laconic bursts of reminiscence.

"Remember the time they sent us to interview Nehru at the airport, and he gave Alice and me a rose?"

"Yes. Poor Alice got so excited she fouled up all her photos."

"And the time I slipped the dirty pun into the etiquette page."

"Schroeder said he came close to hitting a woman that day."

Or David would doze over a book of poetry—dog-eared anthologies mostly: he had never been a very consecutive reader—or they would just sit in the leather chairs until sleep drove them to their cubicles.

One night in her second week, he pretended to read until after she had gone to bed, and she heard the creak of the front door. He came back about two hours later. She listened in the darkness: he was alone. She heard the jingling of his brass bedstead, a descending sigh or two, and then his regular breathing—the rhythm of primitive well-being.

Had he stolen up to the grass huts to find Hadouch? Or taken her into the dunes under the stars? And that smell in the house: obviously the presence of a stranger had created an inconvenience.

A casual bout in the slaves' quarters—that she could swallow. What infuriated her, what left her lying rigid and open-eyed in her bed, was the master's chivalry toward the guest of the plantation. David's needs had always been persistent, predictable; he hadn't been shy about them. She had taken care of them, if not with enthusiasm, at least with competence. She couldn't deny a sneaking curiosity: maybe it would go better now. But her real objective was bigger, and if she started anything herself—even with a flicker of an eyelid—she might drive the game back into the forest.

Shortly after the excursion to the markets, David announced that he was organizing a *dhifa*.

"That's a Moroccan dinner party, isn't it?"

"Right. The *Khalifa* is coming, and a White Russian couple, and a French professor who's stuck it out in Casa. Special dispensation: you can eat with the men. But I warn you: be prepared for seven courses. There'll be pigeon pie, turkey, couscous—the works. And no forks or spoons."

"A *khalifa* must be a caliph. Romantic! But couscous with fingers!"

"And no alcohol to help out. Islam again."

After lunch she heard him giving orders in the lean-to kitchen. Hadouch let loose a flood of comment, in the course of which her voice got rather shrill. There was a sudden, high-pitched syllable from David—he sounded just like an Arab—and a muffled whack, and then silence, followed by stifled sobs.

Victoria didn't budge from her corner. The sound of weeping sickened her with joy. Now was the moment.

She went off to Casablanca the next morning. In the back of her car she decided to carry the big nude, two other portraits in oil, and several of the marine abstracts.

David gave her an encouraging pat on the shoulder, and then withdrew into feigned indifference. So it was Hadouch who helped her load the car. For the first time she gave Victoria a wide smile, and her eyes sparkled, as though the womenfolk had conspired to purify the house by removing graven images.

After the sun-beaten countryside, Casablanca was an irritant, a colonial anachronism, where the Moroccans looked like extras in costume posed against the monuments of Lyautey. Most of the art galleries had disappeared. Those that survived were crammed with expensive shoddy framed in dusty gilt. At Bernaud's the presiding genius was now an Algerian Jew in a morning coat and beret. He sized up Victoria carefully before he agreed to look at the pictures.

Bernaud had retreated to Paris. *"Parti depuis longtemps.* But he still has property here. He comes to Casa now and then."

Victoria asked him to send her greetings. Between them they extricated the big canvases from the car, and then she went to retrieve the smaller things. When she came back, the Algerian was turning the nude this way and that in his hairy little paws, scrutinizing it with evident distaste.

"It would go like hotcakes down here," he sighed.

"But who would buy such things?"

"Chère madame, they're just right for the nouveaux riches who have taken over the big villas. The Moroccan bourgeois imagine they have thrown off the old taboos about alcohol and art, but nothing can rid them of the dreadful taste of the civil servants."

"What would they bring?"

"Say a thousand dinars each, to start with, minus my commission."

"The painter would have to decide for himself, but that's not exactly a fortune."

"No, but from the look of it this chap could turn them out in job lots."

So there it was: respectable, not too unprofitable, but hack-work all the same. Victoria took care to conceal her agreement.

The seascapes got a longer look. "I couldn't handle these."

"You don't find them interesting?"

"Mais si, madame! They're much *too* interesting." A glimmer of enthusiasm pierced the cynical expertise. "There's no market down here any longer, but in Paris perhaps—Why not try M. Bernaud directly?"

"You really think it's worth bothering him?"

"Oh, I'm sure he'd take a look. I could hang one or two here, if you like. Once in a while someone with taste wanders in—from the cruise ships, for instance. But it's a long chance these days."

"I'll have to ask the painter."

He looked at her with a flicker of derision. "Yes, do ask him. Tell him to come out of his cave. I'm available; I won't bite."

Victoria stuffed the canvases into the car. She looked at her watch: only three o'clock, but there was little point in looking elsewhere. She had found the bait she needed.

There was no one in the yard at this hour—only the dogs dozing in the shade—and no sounds from indoors. In the lean-to she saw a huge chunk of lamb, which had begun to draw flies, and a scruffy turkey with its plucked neck hanging over the edge of the sink. But the empty house slumbered in the spell of afternoon. Leaving the paintings in the car, Victoria scrambled to the top of a dune, blinking against the bright sky.

Below the sand bluff David stood at the water's edge. He was naked: even at that distance she could see the startling white of his buttocks below his broad, tanned back. As she watched, he waded slowly toward the foaming line of breakers. Once he stopped for a stretch, spreading his arms high and wide toward the sun.

Even against the tumult of the surf, Victoria could hear her breath coming faster. She could hardly believe that the dark, hairless body, stronger than she remembered and quite unconscious of itself, had the power to churn up such an intensity in her. Was this what all her plans, her expectant patience, had been leading up to?

She fumbled with the buttons of her blouse and was just drawing breath to give him a shout when the grass stirred in the dune to her right. She ducked out of sight as Hadouch and Mehdi went scuffling down the sand bank. The child was naked; the woman wore only a white shift. Darting a glance around her, she dropped it at the water's edge. The boy shrieked like a gull, and the two of them made straight for David, the surf streaming over them as they leaped through the waves.

David plunged. Three long strokes brought him back to where they stood in the shallows. The woman turned away, but he thrust his hand under her arm and, covering her breast, pulled her down to him in the water. He spouted and laughed like a rowdy Triton, and the child looked down at them and laughed too. Then all three joined hands, the boy swinging in the middle, and ploughed toward shore through the swirl of the ebbing tide.

Victoria scuttled back across the dune like a crab and made a crouching dash for the car. Near the grass huts Abdul was heaving tomato baskets into the truck, but he did not turn around. She gunned her motor and careened down the rocky driveway, skidding out onto the main road. When she had driven nearly a mile, she drew up on the dusty shoulder and sat back trembling. Behind her closed eyes the images ballooned: the swinging breasts, David's dark hand, the laughing child.

She struggled out of the car and snatched the big nude from the back. Standing in the dappled shade of a eucalyptus, she held it at arm's length. For a minute she thought of trampling on it and leaving it in the ditch. But in the end she crammed it into the car again and drove slowly back.

David sat on a camp stool in the yard, clean and shining in white ducks and T-shirt, with a small canvas on his knee and his pipe clenched between his teeth. The boy sprawled at his feet, sifting sand through his fingers into little mounds.

"How was the great city?" David asked, without looking up.

"Ghastly. Things have changed all right, and not for the better. I'm really worn out."

"Why don't you sit down a spell?" He squeezed a blob of green onto the canvas. "We've been working on the stuff for the party tomorrow, and supper is nowhere near ready."

"No thanks. I've got to pack."

"Pack?"

"Yes, I stopped at the post office. A letter from Alice: we have to rush off to Cannes to cover some movie thing. So she needs help finishing up Tangier. I'll be leaving first thing in the morning."

He worked on with quick slashing strokes. "I'm sorry. You'll miss the *dhifa.*"

"Damn the *dhifa*! Is that really all you have to say?"

He looked up at last. "You *are* tired. Better go and lie down."

But she was not about to let him off. "Tell me, David, why did you bring me down here?"

"I might better ask why you wanted to see me in Fez."

"Come off it."

"I'm fond of you, Victoria. I enjoy having you around, now that we've nothing to fight about. There's no one down here like you— or like me." He turned the brush slowly on his palm as if he were hefting a knife. "I can't go native all the time."

"Well, you've made a start. Quite a good one, I'd say." She looked off at the undulations of the dunes; their violet edges had softened with a faint foreshadowing of autumn rain. Then her glance fell on Mehdi. "I suppose you couldn't bear my not knowing."

He got up quickly, jabbing the handle of his brush into the sand. The boy gave a little whimper and darted across the yard to the kitchen. "What did you expect?" David said. "Sir Galahad? My requirements may not be as complicated as yours, but they're real enough."

"That's a low blow, David." She fought against the tremor in her voice. "I was stupid enough in Fez to hope that things might go better for us. But in that direction, you never gave me any chance."

After a bit he said more calmly, "Well, you know how I am. I guess I'd never be happy in a pond if I could find a puddle."

"You needn't worry."

"Are you saying you had no luck with the pictures?"

"On the contrary, the trip was very interesting."

He turned sharply. "You found someone for the seascapes?"

His lighted face checked her: had she any right to exploit his hopes? But when she caught in his eye a gleam of the old hang-dog deference, her vanity flamed up again. "Not exactly. Outdoor work is not really your thing, it seems."

"You can't mean that Bernaud liked the figures better."

"Bernaud has copped out. He's left Morocco, but I showed all the stuff to another dealer. He thought the marine canvases were very nice in their way, but— "

"Oh nice, nice! The hell with that. I thought you liked them."

"I do like them, myself."

"Well then?"

"They don't quite work. They don't grow on me. Too many people do the geometric act nowadays. I'd stick to the figures. They're bread and butter, after all, and more than that, they're good. Some day you may be famous."

"It's kind of a waste of time if no one is going to like the things I like."

Just the gambit she had hoped for—but now it was too late. "I may be mistaken," she said slowly, driving the last nail, "but that's how I see it."

"Thanks, Victoria. You sure tried." His hand rested lightly on her shoulder. "Look, I'm sorry that—well, that things didn't work out. Honestly."

She couldn't trust herself to say another word. The mirror had cracked all right, she told herself as she turned to go into the house, and no knight had looked her way.

From inside the doorway, she saw David crossing the yard. He opened the back of the car and, pushing aside the smaller canvases, carefully lifted out the largest. Holding it at arm's length in the waning light, he gave it the first kind scrutiny it had received that day.

The Bigger Thing

In the long succession of domestics with whom we were blessed—or afflicted—in the Foreign Service, Julian figures as the only one we neither hired nor fired. We paid his wages, but he was a fixture in the white brick house assigned to us in The Hague. He was mentioned with awe by preceding counselors and with warbles of enthusiasm by their wives. Even the Post Report, that most impersonal of documents, carried a brief anonymous reference, as though a British butler had been installed in the Sophialaan along with the American iceboxes and heating plant. After one had become familiar with the decent old house, one could as little imagine it without Julian as without the immemorial oak in the garden or the darkly gleaming green door which Julian had opened to guests for nearly twenty years.

My wife and I had not looked forward to our encounter with this immovable personage. Even if Julian proved complaisant, we foresaw him as venerable, white-haired, tottery on the stairs perhaps, or shaky with trays and messages. And if we were to propose any change of personnel, no doubt we would be considered heretical if not inhuman.

As luck would have it, we passed through The Hague before our assignment was announced and got a chance to spy out the land at a party given by my predecessor. It turned out quite unlike other diplomatic crushes: no stale, curling sandwiches; no frantic, high-keyed chatter; only the comfortable hum of those who were properly ministered to. A bald automaton in a wing collar circulated champagne; a Frisian girl with yellow hair and flaming cheeks trotted about with hot canapés. But they both wore the withdrawn and bewildered air that marks the tribe whose members "come in to help out." It took a few minutes to discern the true center of control.

"But he's not old at all!" my wife suddenly exclaimed. "He can't be a day over forty."

As she spoke, I made out a brisk, diminutive figure in a white coat fastened by two brass buttons on a cord. His wavy ginger hair was slicked down flat; his round face, freckled and a bit liverish, wore the serene smile of authority. He paced his station like a captain on the bridge, occasionally leaving the dining-room door to direct the disoriented or to break up traffic jams in the receiving line. Now and then, in response to some signal invisible to me, he would glide up to our host and, standing on tiptoe, whisper in his ear. I noted that whenever Julian bore a hand with the trays, he concentrated on those groups where heads drew closest in conversation.

When the company had dwindled to the hard kernel of lingerers, our host found a minute to introduce us. Julian's handshake was dry and firm; his tone was chirpy rather than servile; his accent was dimly cockney. He told us that when he was barely twenty, he had come to the Sophialaan through one of those postwar flukes that followed the Liberation. He had cut short his career as a steward in the British Navy to marry in Holland.

"You live out then?" asked my wife.

"Yes, madam, I leave after dinner. Except of course whenever you need me."

My wife nodded at me: "whenever" sounded generous.

Later my host drew me aside. "There's just one thing you should watch out for."

"Oh?"

"The new Ambassador's wife has her eye on Julian. I don't know how far Mrs. Spear will go, but I know Julian."

"You mean he'll desert us?"

"On the contrary. He'll count on you to resist."

2

Americans chafe under the bonds of master and servant, but Julian came to see us, in the months that followed, less as bosses than as subjects. Not that he dominated our lives—no one could have resembled less the domestic bully of popular legend; rather, he viewed us as a diplomat views the interests he accommodates. Even the chauffeur Joop, although not under Julian's orders, was permeable to his influence, especially since they shared a passion for auto racing. Julian's cockney croonings also soothed the tantrums of our French cook Marguerite—"Mag," as he called her—although his loyalty could not conceal her lapses, which were infrequent but total. For one large dinner Mag had riveted her attention so firmly on a superb *boeuf à la mode* that she forgot all the vegetables. When my wife rang her little silver bell, which she rarely had to do, Julian's face, white with humiliation, popped around the edge of the Chinese screen. "Carrots out," he whispered. "Beans next time around." He changed our plates presently and brought the beans, crunchy but delicious, on a silver platter, held aloft so as to demonstrate that at our table, as in France, vegetables were worthy of separate consumption.

Julian's own skills ran to American cocktails and what he called "clever cold bits." Households of American children, including our own on their rare visits, had inured him to hamburgers, but he drew the line at un-American simplicities. When Marguerite conspired with us to serve *brandade* of codfish to luncheon guests, Julian did not conceal his opinion of this pungent dish. "It smells like cat piss—sir."

His talent for solving—or softening—others' problems, whether decrepit sports cars or deficient memories, no doubt explained his appetite for diplomacy. The mention of ambassadors always brought light to his blue eyes; he knew them all—including their warts. Once the barriers of reserve between us had lowered, he shared his penchant for wicked nicknames. The Swiss Ambassador, who suffered from the double handicap of conjunctivitis and pomposity, was baptised "Old Sheep's Eyes." The Hungarian, a smarmy and mean-tongued veteran of cold-war diplomacy, was "Count Dracula." The dean of the corps, a wiry, muttering Mexican, spinner of endless intrigues over precedence and farewell cigarette boxes, was carried on Julian's rolls as "the Spider." But the Italian, who always left double tips on the salver, which is standard equipment in Dutch front halls, was "a perfect gentleman unlike some as might be mentioned."

Julian's real interests, however, were more elevated, his antennae more selective. Wherever voices lowered to the whispers of secrecy or anecdote tapered down to its spearpoint, there our butler was sure to gravitate. As the climax of a confidence approached, it amused me to watch the dilatory zeal with which Julian poked up the fire or measured out brandy or plucked the coffee cups one by one from the tables. Even when pretexts for lingering ran out, he usually reappeared in time for the punch line. The only time I saw his face darken with displeasure was when one of the waiters who "came in" put a query about wine while Julian was serving a salmon mousse to one of the Secretaries of the Royal Household. "Pour it and get on with it," he muttered in accents of stone. I recalled later that the Secretary, with rare indiscretion—perhaps stimulated by Julian's old-fashioneds—had just then been regaling the table with a tale of the Saudi Arabian monarch's bewilderment among the cozy domesticities of royalty at Soestdijk.

During postmortems in the pantry, Julian would interrupt the silent polishing of glasses to share his *ragots* with me, occasionally looking sideways at me to see if I showed surprise. "Quite a shame, sir, about the Spaniard's transfer." Or "Too bad, all the shouting about Cambodia. But I shouldn't worry, sir, if I was you. You should have heard the Dutch slanging the British about Indonesia when first I came here." Sometimes he passed along more startling tidbits. After the Soviet move into Czechoslovakia, he had come upon the Soviet and Polish ambassadors in our garden. "Behind the oak tree, it was. Crikey! A regular Donnybrook. And then old Dracula moved in. Backed the Pole into a corner, they did." This confirmed our impression of rifts among the marauders of the Warsaw Pact.

While our guests had long since accepted Julian as a colleague, I had occasional twinges of uneasiness when I thought of the exploits of "Cicero" in Ankara. My liking for Julian reinforced my abhorrence for the sharp, unthinking cogs of security, but when an eager junior officer mentioned our butler's tendency to "tune in," I agreed to check the files.

The examination was reassuring: an uneventful youth in the East End; honorable discharge from Her Majesty's Navy; small properties in Spain and Holland; twenty unruffled years in the Sophialaan. The only racy bit was that his wife, whose name was Beppie and to whom he had not yet introduced us, had started her career as a striptease artist.

I saw, as I closed the file, that I was dealing not with a spy or a vulgar snoop, but with a diplomat who had tailored his career to the contour of his talents. In other embassies he might have enjoyed darker excitements and higher pay, but except with the British, whom he considered tame, the language barrier would only have frustrated his participation. I liked to think of him as a diplomat of the golden age, an inglorious (but far from mute) Cambon rather than a Venetian slyboots.

3

The cloud of which my predecessor had warned me presently assumed dimensions larger than those of a man's—or in the event, a woman's—hand.

Joseph Spear, the new Ambassador, was a Chicago lawyer in his early forties, with a rubicund, boyish face and the hearty confidence of a Republican problem-solver. He entertained a genial contempt for Foreign Service officers, whom he regarded as "soft on communism" and inclined to long hair. To the sinuosities of foreign ministries he preferred the bluff ultimatums of Chicago's Tribune Tower; though this did him no great harm with the Dutch, it became clear that the piloting of jets pleased him more than the perusal of tedious despatches, and baloney sandwiches in a duck blind more than a garnished table. But while the Ambassador vaguely sensed that the wheels of amenity were better oiled in the Sophialaan ("Your wife is such an old pro"), it was the Ambassadress who descried the central spring of the mechanism.

Cecilia Spear was a Texan of unbounded wealth and imposing stature. Her tightly waved auburn hair and square-cut features recalled the jack of spades. Her dresses and her jewelry, authentic even to the diamond blossoms on her ample shoes, assorted well with the ambassadorial Residence. This was a vast structure of raw brick, dating from Marshall Plan days, when American hegemony demanded greater splendor than the old house in the Sophialaan could supply. In Mrs. Spear's salons the curtains shone like the satins of Copley; the carpets came up to one's shoe tops; the brown-gravy paintings reflected the glitter of a thousand prisms.

Dutch merchants and bankers smiled at all the newness, and the staff did nothing to dampen their mirth. The butler was a darting homosexual (Julian told me that auxiliary waiters at receptions often brought flowers to the back door). The "chef," a cheerful pirate in a white hat, alternated Dutch dishes of no savor whatever (*"Incolore et inodore"* was the French Ambassador's verdict) with Javanese specialties that took the roof off one's mouth. The two of them robbed the iceboxes and cellars with impunity, partly because servants were in short supply and partly because, fearing the repercussions of change on our own domestic bliss, I conspired with the administrative people to cover their tracks. But Cecilia Spear soon discovered that her guests, unlike ours when Julian closed the door after them, did not exchange the glances that meant *"Et in Arcadia ego."*

Though far from timid, the Ambassadress did not attack head-on. Her husband had inculcated a wholesome terror of the nest of vipers into which they had fallen, and Mrs. Spear did not intend to alienate the juniors until she had mastered the vagaries of official hospitality. The opening gambit was a telephonic appeal—an emergency at the Residence: two hundred guests, a sick butler, and the prestige of the U.S.A. And then the shrill and languid accents of Dallas: "Oh would you-all—could you-all—spare your Julian?" Just a few little hours, and he would be returned unharmed and with her undying gratitude. I said I would have to ask Julian, a formality that seemed to surprise her.

When I had hung up, my wife and I looked at each other. How in the name of common solidarity (not to mention the box in my annual rating marked "cooperation") could we refuse? I hoped Julian might say "nothing doing," but of course he didn't. His good nature was unbounded—and I think he saw a chance to show up the Ambassador's staff. I patted him lightly on the shoulder and assured him that the assignment was momentary, temporary, even unique. "Oh I'm sure of that, sir," he said. "As you know, this house is home to me."

So I stood warned. But as I watched the small figure walking briskly down our gravel walk, with his white coat folded over his arm, I felt like a parent who, in sending his child off to a new school, disguises ordeals to come as fun and games.

When my wife received a second S.O.S. a few weeks later, Julian wrinkled his snub nose and reminded her that we were giving a big dinner that night. Then the Ambassador, in some embarrassment, took it up with me. This time I returned a *fin de non recevoir.* (Julian would have approved of that term: he loved the diplomatic jargon and once referred to an expelled Romanian as "persona non-gratified.") Cecilia Spear's manner, when next we met, could only be described as smoldering. And presently she set into motion forces which reduced our household problems to mere flotsam on the tidal wave of administrative disaster.

In the meantime Julian himself provided a respite by falling violently ill. He had suffered for weeks, but clenched his teeth and said nothing, until one evening, while serving the soup, he doubled up over a chair amid a clatter of chinaware. The empirics into whose hands he was delivered by socialized medicine said it was his biliary duct, although his digestion, already sapped by Spanish and Dutch deep-frying, did not rally to their remedies.

When we visited him in the crowded ward, we saw that Julian's freckles had become more prominent in his pale face, the lines around his mouth more deeply sculptured. To one arm was taped a plastic tube through which dextrose trickled from overhead; the other was blue-dotted from the injection of morphine. But he managed a whispered reply to my wife: "It's not bad right now, madam, but"—he smiled faintly—"it's no bank 'oliday either."

Our halting exchange was interrupted by the arrival of Julian's wife, to whom he at last introduced us. I had expected slinky opulence, but the ex-stripper turned out to be a brawny matron, half a head taller than Julian. Her connections with the theater were apparent only in an elaborate turban clamped down on golden ringlets, and a fluent but unreliable English. "So kindly of Madam and Sir to come," she kept saying.

One morning, when Julian had long since broken the hospital record for the intravenous consumption of dextrose, I arrived to find his bed empty. The ward nurse handed me a shakily penciled note: "Dear Mr. and Mrs. B: An unquiet night. They are taking me to Emergency. No visit today. Yours ever, Julian."

Yours ever! I immediately phoned our own doctor, a small, birdlike man named Popak-Samuels, who loved to make house calls ("so much more congenial!"), did all his own technical work ("Hang it, where do I put this electrode?"), and was recognized as a diagnostic wizard. I could hear him pecking away at ethical questions, and then he said, "After all, I've known the dear fellow at your house for years and years. Nothing to prevent a friendly visit."

The friendly visit included discreet inquiries that boosted Julian's prestige with the hospital staff. And when no one was looking, Dr. Popak rolled back Julian's eyelids, laid a cold, attentive ear to his abdomen, and tweaked his toes reassuringly. "Not biliary," he told me later. "Pancreas. Definitely. I've dropped a hint. I might say the Swedish Ambassador survived the same thing." I said that this last bit might do more good than medicine, but Dr. Popak had already informed the patient.

Little by little Julian began to mend. The Italian Ambassador, blessed man, came by for a visit that consisted mostly of pregnant pauses. And then came the day when Julian requested reading matter. "Oh Mrs. B., if you could just ask Joop to bring around the auto-racing magazines." My wife burst into tears.

During the weeks of convalescence, engagements were taboo. "Doctor's orders," I told Cecilia Spear crisply. At Julian's first reappearance, our guests crowded around him as though he were the star of the Ajax Football Club. Julian, for whom diplomacy was ever the golden mean, presently withdrew to the pantry, his eyes a bit moist. He got back just in time to tune in on an account of General de Gaulle's view of the Dutch, which he played back for me in the pantry. "Pig-headed, tight-fisted, and always with an eye on the main chance. In short, a nation!"

"Quite a compliment," said Julian.

4

One morning—it was just before our transfer back to Washington —my secretary tiptoed in from the outer office, closed the door, and looked around her with the air of one who had fallen into the clutches of a conspiracy.

"They're selling the house," she gasped.

At first I didn't take it in. "Selling what house, Thelma?"

"Your house, Mr. B. The house in the Sophialaan." She planted a white-knuckled fist on my desk. "I overheard the Administration people in the cafeteria. It's an economy move."

"Economy!" My voice rose. "Why don't they sell that goddamned Residence?"

Thelma backed away, her pearl-studded glasses on their chain whacking against her bosom. "No one will buy it. Mrs. Spear *wanted* to sell it. She wanted your place." My secretary snickered. "She was planning to redecorate it from top to bottom."

I dropped back in my chair, a shattered man. "Cecilia Spear. But what in the world—? Thelma, find out when the Ambassador can see me, will you?"

The Ambassador waved me to the visitor's sofa and settled a bit nervously on the edge of his functional desk chair. He fingered a bronze model of Lockheed's latest offering while he explained with breezy gusto the consequences of retrenchment. "Low profile, you know." In Paris they were moving back into the old Rothschild house; in Oslo the Nobel mansion was up for grabs. And so on. The Hague must do its bit. And it was our house that was to be sold.

"No one wants the Residence. Everyone likes your place better— more historical, I guess."

I saw a ray of hope: I reminded him that part of our house was a classified monument.

But Joseph Spear dismissed the centuries with a flip of the hand. "The Foreign Ministry has given the green light. In Holland money casts its shadow—even when the sun isn't shining. We've been offered half a million for it."

"Half a million guilders?"

"Dollars." He smiled craftily. "Still confidential: it's an American buyer. Tappan Petroleum. It's their man for the whole of Europe."

"You know the buyer, Mr. Ambassador?"

His red face turned slightly redder. "He's an old friend. But it's a real good deal for the U.S. government." He looked at me as though I were a troublesome minority stockholder. "Now we wouldn't dream of disturbing you or your wife," he said soothingly. "You'll stay put until you leave for Washington. The next Counselor will get one of those red-brick jobs in Wassenaar—the ones we bought up after the war. Cecilia tells me they're real cozy."

I had a brief, appalling vision of Marguerite in a postage-stamp kitchen and Julian in a snug parlor, circulating lasagna and green salad to guests who were seated on the floor. "We'll have to get rid of the staff," I said. "I ought to tell them right away."

The Ambassador rose and paced restlessly; my despair had thrown him off balance. "Don't let's be precipitate," he said, with a slight tremolo. "Cecilia and I have decided that under the circumstances the least we can do is to offer jobs to your staff."

"All of them, Mr. Ambassador?"

"All." He looked at me and looked away. "Now I'm sure you'll admit that's fair enough."

"Who's to say what's fair? There's Julian, for instance. It will break his heart."

"My wife," said the Ambassador stiffly, "has handled servants all her life."

"That's not what I meant at all. It's just that Julian won't transplant. You might as well try to move the oak out of our garden."

"But that's our life," Joseph Spear told me blandly, as though he had served abroad for a generation. "I wasn't happy to leave Winnetka, and Cecilia still hankers for Dallas."

I flung myself into one last appeal. "It really won't work, Mr. Ambassador. Without the house Julian will go straight downhill—and without Julian, the household will collapse. It just won't work out at all."

For a few seconds he wavered. But then I sensed the shadow of Cecilia Spear; thoughts of vengeful Juno stiffened Jupiter's spine.

"If your man doesn't want the job, that's his own lookout."

5

Julian took it better—and worse—than I had expected. It was the day after our last party (everything had gone like clockwork) and we were standing under the old oak, from which a July windstorm had torn away one branch in the night; above us, the great, livid wound still glistened. More than ever I dreaded my return to the drudgery of Washington desk work. And more and more Julian's lower lip curled over his upper as the implications of our departure dawned.

"The new ones, sir: Tappan. Are they diplomatic?"

"No. Oil."

"Oil? Crikey! Well, I suppose I can give it a whirl."

I shook my head slowly. "They're old friends of the Spears. And Mrs. Spear, as you know, is counting on you for the Residence."

"Crikey!" said Julian again.

"Do you have anything saved up, Julian? Perhaps if you could wait a little—"

"Oh no, sir. What with doctors and the place in Spain, I haven't a bean. I'll have to find something fast—get a move on. Of course now if you was to recommend anyone—"

The great question hung in the air, but I knew I had to shoot it down. Our service in Washington—not to mention the pay—wouldn't do at all. And the unspoken offer was designed to assuage my distress as much as his, for when I said nothing, he added, "I suppose Beppie wouldn't be happy outside Holland."

"There's nothing for it, Julian," I said. "Believe me, I've tried. The Ambassador is a decent fellow—very generous. And Mrs. Spear—well, you'll get on all right. You've had more complicated problems here, I'm sure."

It was then that Julian made the little speech—a long one for him—that remains with me still.

"I know how you take it, sir, you and Mrs. B.and all you done for me. I'm most attached, sir, if I may say so. There's not many as would feel badly like you. But for me, you see, it's a bit worse. This place, and all the people coming and going—well, it's just everything." I could hear the tears rising in his voice. "You've other places to go, some of 'em worse than Holland, I shouldn't wonder. Still you always go where people work—well, on the bigger thing, if you know what I mean. But me"—Julian leaned against the old tree, and his voice flattened out again, without bitterness, to the level of the inevitable—"for me, it's a bit like the Navy: I go below again. And below I expect I stay."

I put my arm around his shoulders. It was no time for cheery afterthoughts.

6

Since The Hague was a favored spot for lawyers and conferences, I came out a year later as a paper-chaser for an oversized and otiose delegation to a petroleum conference. I thought more about Julian than about my colleagues at the green table, but it was awkward to visit him. I didn't burn for a tête-à-tête with Cecilia Spear, and yet I couldn't slip in at her back door with the milkman. At last a reception at the Residence gave me a chance to sneak out to the kitchen, where, to my surprise, I found only our old cook. Marguerite informed me, with downcast eyes that discouraged further questions, that Julian was no longer in the Ambassador's service.

Cecilia Spear confirmed that it hadn't worked out. "I'm afraid," she said in sweet-and-sour tones, "that you all spoiled him."

Joseph Spear was less censorious. "Poor little fellow: he took to nipping in the pantry. Claimed it helped his pancreas. It's funny; we hiked his pay and gave him a regiment of waiters to order around. But he said it didn't raise the tone—whatever that means."

I could have told the Ambassador—but I didn't—that the number of cupbearers was not important. For Julian the sparkle had to extend beyond the champagne.

I inquired in vain for him at the Embassy. And then the Tappan people gave a dinner for the delegation. In the Sophialaan, I found what I had dreaded: an interminable hour swilling cocktails, a grandiose dinner, heavy cooking and heavier shoptalk about the iniquities of the oil-producing countries. But when I looked up from scooping out an unripe avocado, I found a familiar figure in my line of vision across the carnations and the candles.

Julian looked shrunken. His eyes were a bit bleary, and his face was glazed with the boredom of the unattached. His white waistcoat, to which Beppie had affixed a neat patch, and his snap-on tie proclaimed that he had joined the ranks of the anonymous who "come in" to help out. A little later he would drain the wine bottles with the other subalterns; his palm, like theirs, would be crossed with guilders from the salver in the hall. As I looked around at my senior colleagues, I felt that Julian and I had ended up in the same boat. And when his glance intersected mine, he gave me the smile of Talleyrand masquerading at the Feast of the Federation. "Don't look too hard," he seemed to say. "Don't make me laugh."

By the time I had escaped from brandy and cigars and made my way to the vast old pantry, I was too late. "Just left, sir," Julian's successor told me. "Anything I can do?"

When I had sent my kindest regards, I went slowly back to the living room. I thanked my lucky stars that at least Julian would not have to open the front door to let me out.

Concert

The languid strings do scarcely move!
The sound is forced, the notes are few!
—Blake

When Ray Adams bends to his guitar, he spills over the edges of the chair which, during the long year, has come to be recognized as his own. The Chippendale back and delicate legs suggest the salon of a countess or a shipowner, and Inger, looking up from her German phrase book, wonders through what seamy auction rooms, what twists of the downward path, the chair may have passed to end in her uncarpeted walk-up. In its own way it seems as incongruous as Ray himself.

Tonight, again, Ray has come alone. He is clearly relieved that Torbiorn Kristiansen and the other Committee members have not showed up. Inger knows that he is just as uncomfortable with them as he is with his friend Little Joe and the other Americans, black and white, who drop in to sprawl in corners, while coffee simmers on the electric ring, and conversation flickers and flares through the screen of alien language and alien experience.

But tonight there is no palaver about Vietnam or NATO, and Ray can scratch away at his guitar without fear of being importuned. Now and then a string of low velvety notes bubbles from his throat. And all the time he watches Inger, as though she would fade away with the twanging of the strings if he did not keep an eye on her.

Inger has come to dread these solitary visits, but she would be lost without them. She dreads the footsteps echoing on the stone staircase, the gleaming black face, the whites of his eyes rolling at her.

And as the erotic twilight of Nordic summer sets in, she dreads the lunges of desire—the great frame straining against her and the warm hands fumbling at her clothes—that always mark the end of an evening. At these moments Inger, despite deep longing, resists; she takes refuge behind a second virginity, knowing that its loss would be the confession of her own apostasy.

Tonight she would like to be alone, quite alone, with no intruder to burden the Chippendale chair and no strange sounds or thoughts to crowd in upon her. She wants to lie down in the tiny alcove between the coarse sheets, spread her blonde hair on the pillow, close her eyes, and start sorting out her troubles.

Troubles—well, there are plenty of them. Threats of violence have fouled the preparations for the autumn peace rally. Committee members no longer accept evenings of discussion; they want to break windows, throw Molotov cocktails, and chain themselves to fences. There has been a tussle with the police in front of Committee headquarters, and a clash with the Pacifist Peoples Youth on the very day of Indochina Solidarity. One of the boys, the real brain of the Out-of-NATO group, has been caught pushing marijuana in the park behind the Palace. And Inger's own language studies are going down a path whose end is marked "failure."

Worst of all is the anonymous letter in the Committee chairman's mailbox. There it lies molding, like some toxic fungus; when the chairman returns from Helsinki, it is bound to come to light.

With a shake of her head, Inger tries to efface these blots from the canvas of her militancy. She gets up from the couch and puts the graniteware coffeepot on the ring.

"How did it go today?" she asks. This is the invariable opening gambit.

"Nothin' new," Ray tells her. "Nothin' much." This too is classic. But tonight, after a few plinks of the guitar, he adds, "I hear we gotta go to camp."

"Camp?" Inger keeps her voice even, and her English loses nothing of its propriety. "I would say *that* was something new. What sort of camp is it?"

"Dunno. Special camp. Gonna teach us the language. Maybe get us a job. Got to be away for a while, though."

"Where?"

"Up north somewhere."

"Ah, that must be the new reception center for foreigners." Inger explains: "It is an idea of the Social Ministry. You do not *have* to go of course. And no one will force you to learn the language. Still, I suppose it is rather a decent idea."

"I reckon." Ray gives her a half-smile that means total indifference.

She feels a little skip of hope, but fear also rises slowly along her throat.

"When would you go?"

"Sometime soon. Little Joe goin' too. He think it's great."

As she subsides behind her German book, Ray thrums loudly across all four strings. His voice soars in a wordless lament.

Songs with social content please Inger more. She admires Joan Baez and can even sing a few bars of "Mr. President." But Ray will not play the accompaniment. In fact, nearly all the Americans are bored by these battle cries. Although Vietnam is surely their problem as much as it is hers, the war never figures at all in the howling and beating of feet that Ray and Little Joe enjoy the most.

But Inger says nothing. She avoids anything that would offend the Americans or drive them away. That would be counterrevolutionary. Anyway, she and her friends are a bit wary of confronting the blacks. Torbiorn Kristiansen will argue with them, as he will with anybody, in that dry courtroom voice of his. But the others hesitate. It takes nerve to face down the foreigners. And this special breed, with their subterranean passion for razors and revolvers—how can anyone tell what paroxysms they might deploy if some well-meaning stranger were to lean on the hidden button?

So the girls stick to safer subjects whose edges have been dulled by discussion. They chatter shyly of imperialism, the evils of NATO, apartheid, resistance in Portugal, in Spain, in Greece. Sooner or later most of them offer their blue-veined breasts and long flanks, hoping to quiet the leather-coated monsters for whom the Committee has ordered the faithful to assume so many responsibilities. Inger, however, has shrunk from this final tribute.

Thanks to Torbiorn and Inger, one of the condemned frame buildings in the old town has been turned into a dormitory, hung with antiwar posters and curling photographs of Che Guevara and Rudi Dutschke. But so far as Inger can make out, Ray spends little time in this musty edifice. He shuttles back and forth between the Studenterlund and the Alien Police, thrusting his phony passport under the noses of embarrassed civil servants, peeling off meal tickets at the university canteen, scrounging coffee from Inger, and sleeping around with her friends. Boredom, working its way up through every layer of his face, lies heavy on his eyelids and at the corners of his purple mouth.

Whenever Inger thinks about Ray's departure, she foresees an aching emptiness, but relief too, as when a troublesome molar has been torn out. Meantime she knows her duty: to help all those who struggle against the war. The Committee has laid down the line, and Inger, like all the Comrades—except Torbiorn—is undyingly wedded to the "other America." If Ray is not the other America, then who is? So she obeys the commandment of Lenin: to explain and explain again. This and the pouring of endless cups of coffee are her contributions.

One awkward thing: Ray Adams has never been in Vietnam. Three of the white sailors have done duty in the Gulf of Tonkin, and Little Joe has been in Okinawa. But Ray has never done anything except tinker with radios and play the guitar. He has never been east of Kaiserslautern, where he is no doubt carried as AWOL. He has told Inger quite casually that he is wanted for handling stolen goods: transistors and tax-free whisky from the PX. (Though she hates herself for doing it, Inger occasionally checks the knickknacks of ornate silver and the handmade brooch that her parents gave her when she left the Gudbrandsdal for the university two years ago.) The more active Americans have ground a few revolutionary phrases into Ray, just to keep him respectable. Once in a while he mutters about "victims of napalm" and "wars of liberation," and he knows about

Angela Davis and the Soledad Brothers. But only last week he balked at marching in the torchlight parade that wound up the week of Vietnam Solidarity.

"My feet get tired, girl." (He never uses Inger's name.) "Anyway, I done my bit when I finked out in Germany. You-all told me so yourself."

"But you must keep on, Ray. There is so much more to do."

"Keep on? You think it's easy, what I done? You ought to see them stockades sometime. You don' know ol' Sergeant Paul in our outfit. Feel that rifle butt in your gut. Man, oh man!"

But in all this chop-licking terror, Inger hears an undertone of nostalgia.

"We all must help each other," she tells him. "Otherwise the war could go on forever."

"Ain't my war, girl. I got my own little war—right here." He chuckles as his eyes fasten on the great breasts under her gray sweater. "Maybe we could use a little combat duty, honey? Or maybe I show you how to sign the peace?"

When she hears such talk, Inger clenches her teeth, as though she were a nun who despairs of works without faith. "I am no good," she tells herself. "I have not applied the principles correctly."

She bends over her German book in a frenzy of concentration. But the silly phrases slide out from under her eyes. Angily she puts down the book and lifts the pot from the ring.

But as she pours the umpteenth cup, she longs to slip away down the damp staircase with its smell of carbolic, and out into the sweet summer evening. She dreams of sitting again on the bench near the quay, with birch leaves rustling overhead and the blue of night slowly deepening in sky and water. And if she stared long enough at the first star, Torbiorn might slide quietly onto the seat and plant a cold kiss on her mouth. That would simplify many things.

If only she could fit life back into neat compartments: hours of "philo" and the growing mastery of German, evening Committee sessions in the Aula, silent marches past the American Embassy with torches and placards, walks in the wood and Torbiorn's hard body pressed against hers in the leaves, her hands in his tight, dark curls. Sighs and shudders and swift stabs of desire; no hunger, no complications.

Then she remembers their last encounter on the steps of the library.

"You are losing your head," Torbiorn had warned her. "You will end with nothing but trouble."

"I have no trouble," she told him. "At least I have no more than you."

"Different for the men." Torbiorn was very lofty. "They don't get involved really. You are too involved."

"You mean I do more."

"More about what?"

"About the war."

"Oh, the war, for God's sake, the Imperialist War." Torbiorn's voice was cold with scorn. "What do any of us way up here at the end of Europe know about the war. None of the Americans is interested in what we think or what we do."

"We have to make them understand then."

"They live off of us, that's all, until they can find somewhere else to go. And most of all they live off you."

"But not off *you*, I notice." Inger's tone was hard and flat. She shook her head so that her taffy hair swung round her shoulders. "Always time for your law books—and your skis, of course. And the girls in the woods."

Torbiorn's eyes rounded. "And what about you? You see nothing but blacks nowadays. The blacks don't need any woods."

"Congratulations! I see you are becoming a racist. The law is doing wonders for you."

"Yes, wonders."

"Does the Committee know how you feel?"

"Screw the Committee."

"Charming thought! Perhaps someone should tell them."

"Blacks, blacks," Torbiorn repeated, with the desperate relish of one who has already gone too far to turn back. "Ignorant blacks. And counterrevolutionary into the bargain. Ray Adams is clearly counterrevoluntionary."

"Racist! Fascist!"

"*Tosk!*" Torbiorn flared out at her. "I suppose you know he sleeps with all your friends as well as you."

Inger raised her hand to her cheek. "I have never slept with Ray Adams," she said.

Torbiorn greeted this with a sharp, dry laugh. For an instant she stood staring at him, biting at her knuckles. Then she swung away and raced up the library steps, her long legs flashing in the sunlight.

There will be a meeting, of course, and then an inquiry, with everyone pledged to secrecy. And then they will convoke Torbiorn for a hearing.

Inger takes refuge in her phrase book: "The ceiling is above; the floor below." "Pardon me." "I am sorry." "You are welcome." "There are seven days and twelve months." "Forgive me." "Never mind."

Ray watches her lips in mild surprise. He starts to get up. "What you sayin', girl?"

But when she give him no answer, he sinks back, the guitar across his knees, teeth flashing, as he yawns into a high-pitched keening that soars above his strumming. He tilts the Chippendale chair, and the spindly legs give a sharp cry. Hypnotized, Inger watches the expanse of dark skin that widens between the cuffs of his khaki trousers, stained with the smut of city streets, and his G.I. shoes, shuffling and shifting on the bare plank.

Tonight for the first time she envies Ray. How lovely to be shipped off to camp, where everyone else takes all the responsibilities and your mind is made up for you. Inger has begun to loathe the endless meetings, where everything is dissected and nothing decided.

Silently she ticks off the watchwords and pops them into pigeonholes: recognize East Germany, liberate Yuri Daniel and Angela Davis, break up NATO, U.S.A. out of Asia. And of course there are Mao and Che Guevara, summer camps in Cuba, the Peruvian Indians, not to mention the Helsinki Principles or the Stockholm Precepts. Inger secretly longs for just a whiff of heresy. But she finds none—only the acrid smoke of burned-out causes among which she must wander uncomforted.

She revolves in her mind various schemes for retrieving the letter, but none of them is any good. Is it still in the tin box where Committee mail accumulates at the top of the Aula stairs? Or has someone already slit it open? She sees the envelope lying on the pitted surface of the chairman's table, while he scans the flimsy notepaper for a clue to the author, rubbing his scruffy beard, his eyes narrowed, his lips gleaming wetly.

She will have to sit through the meeting with the others, her cheeks flaming, while Torbiorn listens to the epithets bouncing around the bare room: "counterrevolutionary"; "racist"; "fascist lackey." She sees Torbiorn pushing his curls brusquely off his forehead, while he reduces the charges to ribbons. Although everyone will hate him for his scornful lawyer's logic, in the end they will have to let him off. But the drop of poison will remain; no one will ever quite trust him again.

As for Inger, Torbiorn will say nothing. But his eyes will fix her with the flash of blue she knows so well. And he will guess—oh, he will guess easily enough—and whenever she sees him she will be pierced by the knife of his contempt.

Ray stops thrumming and lays the guitar on the floor.

"What you think, girl?"

"Think about what?"

"What we gonna do?"

Inger prepares her defenses again. "About what?"

But the evening is full of surprises.

"I mean do you-all think I should go to camp?" He puts his hands on his knees, the palms showing pink and vulnerable at their edges. "Or should I maybe better go back where I come from?"

"To the States?"

"No, not the States, girl. Germany."

"To Germany! But why should you do that?"

"Ain't gonna be no picnic, girl. I know that. But they ain't no one gonna kill me either. Anyhow I'm only twenty-three and I don't reckon to stay around here my whole life."

"But staying here is important, Ray. You help to end a filthy war. You fight for peace."

Ray cannot suppress a smile. Inger senses that for her sake he bites back the great American monosyllable.

"Little Joe, he say all that crap ain't for me. No more meetin's. Action is more my thing. Freak out. Keep movin'! Now what about this camp, girl?"

Inger's ear picks up a tremor in his voice. Tonight he needs a new kind of help. "How can I tell you, Ray?" she says gently. "How do I know?"

"What they gonna do for me I can't get done somewheres else?"

"Maybe we should find out more, Ray. We could take it up with the Committee before we decide."

"'Fore *I* decide," Ray says. "I don't care about no committee. I wanna hear what you think, girl. Tell me now."

"Well, you could learn the language. Then perhaps they would teach you a trade." Ray cocks his head skeptically, but Inger carries bravely on. "Maybe an electrician, or a radioman. Then you could stay here as long as you want, without being always on the drift."

"Without bein' a bum is what I reckon you aim to say, girl." Ray furnishes this gloss with no trace of rancor.

"No, no, Ray. Not a bum, no."

"What you mean, then?"

"I mean you would not be always alone. Not always on the outside."

"Around here," Ray says, in a rare analytic flash, "bein' on the outside is kind of the same as bein' a bum, ain't it?"

He lifts the guitar back onto his lap and plucks hard at a single string. But he does not raise his voice, and his feet are still.

Inger knows that he will not sing to her again. She feels a rush of pity. She recognizes this sentiment as unworthy, but she goes over all the same and sits timidly on the floor, with her shoulders just touching his knees.

Ray's breathing catches a little. "You know how it is, girl," he says; "you must know how it is." He lifts her hair gently from her neck, but not so gently that she misses his rising excitement. "It just ain't right for me up here."

To this Inger finds no answer—how could she really? She leans her head against his knees. She is on the verge of tears. It doesn't matter any more where Ray goes—off to camp or back to Germany, or even to America. It's all the same, really: in the end she has failed. But to let him just fade away—that she cannot bear. The flood of her dismay becomes suddenly a flood of desire.

Ray bends down and his mouth covers hers. This time Inger does not resist. Not at all.

He lifts her easily and carries her to the narrow bed, raising her up like a child to pull her dress over her head. She helps him with her pants. Then his warm hand is all over her belly and breasts.

Ray gets up and she hears the clink of coins and the thump of his shoes. When she turns her head, he is standing with his hand on the back of his chair, naked in the twilight. She sees his big arms and thighs—they are more smoothly carved than she expected—and when he turns toward her, she bites her lips and her eyes close. Then he moves back to the bed and lies down beside her.

Behind Inger's eyelids, little shutters, rushing past in a jagged circle, fly open one by one, framing the sad faces of the Comrades. Torbiorn pops up last, grimacing and laughing soundlessly.

"Forgive me," she whispers. "Help me. Forgive me."

Ray lays a finger on her lips. His other hand reaches around and holds her gently by the neck, like a puppy. "I got nothin' to forgive you for, girl," he says. "Not now."

Inger gives a little murmur, and he crouches above her. The musk of his sweat fills her nostrils, and her hands clutch inadequately at his thighs. She finds herself opening, opening to him in a boundless solace she has never known before. She drifts on a warm, wide sea where no course is charted and she no longer can tell where the shore lies.

In the shadows Torbiorn's lips tremble; his face wavers and melts away.

Her head turns from side to side on the pillow, and the little bed begins to creak. Just then the guitar scrapes against the Chippendale chair; she hears it hit the floor with a hollow *tock* and a jarring of strings.

Inger calls out in terror, as her eyes open to the dark, oblivious face and throat lifting away from her. But her voice is drowned in the hoarse cry that comes from Ray. She flings one arm up and the tide closes over her.

The Sign of the Horns

Burdened as he was, Jean-Baptiste took the village steps downward with caution, keeping to the shady side, avoiding the pellets of sheep dung. In his left hand he clutched a pick. From his neck dangled a string of tiny wicker baskets, each one lined with brown paper. In his right hand he balanced his shotgun with loving ease; under his open corduroy jacket, belts of cartridges bounced gently against his chest. Not even the August heat could separate him from the hunting cap of rabbit fur that he wore slightly askew on his black curls. But until he had delivered the pick and the baskets, he could give no serious thought to the rabbits and partridges out on the moor.

Near the vine-covered porch of the Mayor, he paused to watch the new puppies, silver-age offspring of M. Champetier's spaniel bitch. The old mother growled ritually but did not move. She knew Jean-Baptiste Cabrillac well, and so did Mme. Champetier, who waved briskly from her upper casement.

"But how you are loaded down today, *mon ami!*" she cried.

Jean-Baptiste touched his cap with the barrel of his gun and moved on. Today he had no time for the ceremonial Pastis, which, once offered, could not be refused. Catherine had warned him that the chief of the dig would be waiting for him at the cavern, and, like most of the Americans, Mlle. Pillsbury was apt to get restless. Even more fidgety was her deputy, Clifford Sterrit, who chipped and scraped in the caverns from dawn to dark, shouting orders to the others in jerky French, hurrying off with bits of pottery and bronze to the shepherd's hut, where Catherine Cabrillac's typewriter clicked away the summer hours as she assembled the inventory of the dig.

At the bottom of the steps, Jean-Baptiste passed the last house in Barjaux. It belonged to Amédée and Eulalie Douarnez, who had come to the village, trailing political clouds from the Basque country, when Jean-Baptiste was still a boy. From the Douarnez garden, he could hear a toneless keening, like the shrill of a solitary locust: old Eulalie no doubt, brooding over village scandal or consecrating one of her potions. She concocted her philters from herbs gathered on the moor and sold them to sick or amorous villagers, or to women with "complaints." Ever since he joined the Communist party, Jean-Baptiste had foresworn Eulalie's remedies. He bought his pills from the pharmacy of a Comrade in Avignon, perusing with wonder the lyrics of modern science that were stuffed into the mouths of the bottles. Catherine was less dogmatic: while she laughed at village magic, some impulse of curiosity—perhaps she had caught it from him—sent her on visits to Eulalie's back garden. Jean-Baptiste suspected consultation, especially as three years had passed with no sign of pregnancy. But of this they did not speak.

Today, as he listened to Eulalie's voice, Jean-Baptiste's index and little fingers moved on the stock of his gun. Almost without his thinking, they formed the sign of the horns with which the villagers warded off the evil eye.

Near the river bank he stopped to sniff the breeze that carried the scent of sun-warmed thyme and mint from the moors. Ahead of him stretched the green ribbon of the Cèze, flowing through perspectives of overarching rock and green-gold foliage that reminded him of the gleaming canvas he had once seen in Avignon, in which his homonym baptized Jesus. From the path that led to the caverns, he could see the crude stone dome of the hut rising above the reeds. For once Catherine's typewriter was silent: only the whisper of the river and the rustle of poplars broke the noontime hush.

Suddenly, from behind the reeds, came the high, raucous laugh of a man, and then a softer voice, barely audible. The two sounds flowed along together and then, just as suddenly, they stopped.

Had M. Sterrit found himself a woman?

At the Mickey Bar, where villagers gathered after the *pétanque* matches, Clifford Sterrit was the butt of the sly barbs which the Barjauvians reserved for the sexual relations of archaeologists. So Jean-Baptiste couldn't resist bending down for just a glimpse through the reeds.

At first all he saw was Sterrit's broad, denim-covered back and flaming red hair in the doorway of the hut. His arms were wrapped around a figure hidden in the shadows; his shoulders twisted and turned; his feet shifted in the dust. No words passed, only Sterrit's panting bursts of laughter and the murmur of the woman. When she wriggled out of his grasp and disappeared into the hut, Sterrit turned and crossed the grass till he stood just a few feet from the concealing reeds. His freckled face was wet, his hair in disorder. He fumbled briefly at his groin, and his mouth twisted as though in pain. And just then the dry clickety-click of the typewriter—faltering at first, and then faster—floated out on the summer air.

Jean-Baptiste's face was on fire, but his legs and belly were frozen, as though he had waded into an April freshet. His feet were fixed there at the opening in the reeds. But Sterrit did not see him, and after a minute, without quite knowing how he had moved, Jean-Baptiste found himself again on the path to the caverns. The blood roared in his ears.

Jean Baptiste was thirty-five and Catherine twenty-one; they were the youngest couple left in the village, from which many families had migrated to the factories of Lyon. He had met her at a Communist ball in Avignon when she was still an orphan of the *Assistance Publique*. She had long blond hair and brown, heavy-lidded eyes; her slim boy's body was a far cry from the large-girdled women of Barjaux in their black dresses. The social workers had dragooned her into secretarial courses and found her a job in the offices of a dress factory, from which she played hookey as often as she dared. She was not, Jean-Baptiste soon discovered, one of the Faithful, only a vague hanger-on of the *jeunesse* who smoked pot and thrummed guitars under the plane trees of the Place de l'Horloge and drifted into and out of the lives of other drifters from Paris or the States.

After several waltzes and many Pastis, Jean-Baptiste began to ridicule these bourgeois pastimes. "You're an escapist," he said, and when she answered in cold monosyllables, he said she was imitating Catherine Deneuve. *"Merde,"* she cried, and hit him across the mouth. She left him gaping on the dance floor amid the snickers of the Comrades.

When Jean-Baptiste recovered from his astonishment, he was hooked. The siege lasted for months; in the end he convinced her that anything would be better than the daily grind in the long rows of typewriters. And this bearded villager with his silences and his steady eyes was a novelty after the scruffy, adenoidal boys of the motorcycle set. Catherine shuddered when she first saw the old Cabrillac house, with its blankly staring oval windows in the attic, from which the silkworms had disappeared long ago. But she could see that her stubborn suitor was respected in Barjaux. His was the most telling spin on the silver bowling balls; his the marksmanship most admired on the moors. Everyone told her that he pulled double his weight in the vineyards and in the town council. At the Mickey Bar, all the Comrades agreed that he had a future in the Party.

Jean-Baptiste arranged the marriage at the Mairie of Barjaux. No bans; no curé—only Mayor Champetier, his glasses slipping on his nose, as he lisped out the ceremonial of the Republic. Mme. Casaubon, the doyenne of the village, whispered of disasters to come. "No religion, either of them. And she must be years younger. You saw the friends who came from Avignon! She will not take easily to Barjaux, *cette petite.*" But Jean-Baptiste had been as proud as if he had led the vineyard workers to the barricades.

And yet—what was it? He hadn't expected her to take any interest in politics; he hadn't even confided his dream of becoming Barjaux's first Communist mayor. But even when Catherine clung to him on cold nights in the great oaken bedstead, he sensed a core of resistance he could not touch, a remnant of interrupted youth, like the weeds among the village stones whose leaves came away in one's grasp, leaving the obstinate roots to expand in the dark soil until they were ready to put forth new shoots.

With her back to the rocks, Eugenia Pillsbury, half-camouflaged by brown face and brown felt hat, sat on a campstool, brooding like a sibyl over the bits of pottery laid out on a newspaper at her feet. Jean-Baptiste had often come upon her in this pose. "This is Megalithic," she would say. "See the bell shape: a wine jar. No, that one is not Ligurian at all—not even pre-Roman. Catherine, bring your notebook." That spelled finis to any discussion.

She looked up now, as Jean-Baptiste approached, and her eyes lighted, blue and youthful in her furrowed face. While he laid down his gun and untwisted the necklace of baskets, she ran her long fingers over the edge of the pick. "Perfect. And the baskets—just what we need."

Jean-Baptiste picked up his gun, tossed it and caught the stock lightly, right at the point of balance.

"You had better be careful with that thing," said Mlle. Pillsbury in her flat but easy French. "It's apt to go off, isn't it?"

He sighted along the barrel, while a slow dizziness rose and fell behind his eyeballs. "I've been carrying shotguns all my life."

"You are going to the moor? What's for supper tonight: rabbit or partridge?"

"If I have any luck—" He broke off with a sharp little laugh. Then he said, "You must tell no one."

"The season has not opened, I take it."

He passed his hands over the cartridge belts under his jacket. "The moor is not small. If I stumbled over a rabbit, my gun, as you say, might go off."

Mlle. Pillsbury returned his wink. "Next week," she said, "I wonder if you could look around in Avignon for something else. For the bronze fragments I need wooden boxes, about like so"—she held up her leathery hands—"and with covers lined with cotton, if you can manage."

"I shall find them. Will you finish the digging soon?"

"But we have finished. At least down here. The last thing will be the cavern behind Mme. Casaubon's melon patch. We must get everything done before the frost. But first I need a few days for myself, just to sort out what we've already found. So everyone will have a vacation—except me. Sterrit and the others leave for Avignon tonight."

There was a long southern silence. Then Jean-Baptiste said, "He is going for good, M. Sterrit?"

Something in his tone made Mlle. Pillsbury look up. The deadening of his eyes was disconcerting. "Only for ten days. But don't worry: I'll see that he leaves money for all those purchases with your wife. M. Sterrit is sometimes careless."

"You are expecting my wife?"

"Oh, an hour ago. But they have a lot to do down there at the hut. It's no joke, you know, getting five thousand years down on paper."

"I shall leave you now," said Jean-Baptiste abruptly, "if you need nothing more."

Eugenia Pillsbury watched him climb the path to the moors until his fur hat, bobbing above the bushes, disappeared around the first bend. Not for the first time, she wondered how this village Rousseau figured her role among the outlanders. His shy speech betrayed no bigotry like that of Mme. Casaubon and nothing of Eulalie Douarnez's mystic grumbling. But his devotion to the village couldn't be questioned. Catherine was different: her job with the Americans was an escape hatch rather than an opening to unknown dangers. Yet she felt tenderness for Catherine even when she teased her.

"You're the only career woman in Barjaux," she told her once. "And doesn't M. Cabrillac object to your working for the imperialists?"

Catherine was tone-deaf to irony and at times brutally explicit. "Jean-Baptiste will not mind so long as the checks pile up in the kitchen drawer. He can use them."

"But when we have packed up and gone, he will haul you back to your kitchen by your hair."

Catherine had laughed rather uncomfortably. "Let us not speak of it."

Sprawled under a scrub oak, with the wind of the moors in his ears and his rabbit hat pulled over his eyes, Jean-Baptiste tried to piece together some plan, some remedy. But always he came back to a vision of the wet mouth, and the freckled hands blindly pawing at Catherine in the shadows of the hut. He heard again the reckless laugh and the answering murmurs.

Gradually his rage sharpened its focus. His wife, he told himself, was not a whore. There had been other men before him, of course, in the gardens and grubby hostels of Avignon, but the real fires hadn't touched her. And now she had been abused. His anger with Sterrit mounted into yellow fury against all the invaders: the Dutch, who disfigured the hills with a rash of stucco villas; the Swiss, who closed their shutters and fled at the approach of autumn; the Parisians, who fouled the summer air with the stink and whine of motorbikes. And now the Americans, careless and arrogant and full of sweet talk that meant nothing.

Catherine did not come home that night. When Jean-Baptiste straggled in from the moor, he found his basset hound whimpering to be let out and a pot of soup scummed over on the stove. A note on the mantelpiece announced her departure: "for a few days," it said, but there was no explanation. The jar in the kitchen dresser was nearly empty of coins; the checks had gone from the drawer. When he climbed to their attic bedroom, with the basset galumphing behind him, her clothes lay in disorder at the bottom of the armoire; her blue jeans were missing.

The chatter in Barjaux did not remain underground for long. Jean-Baptiste put it about that Catherine had been called back to Avignon by sickness in her brother's family. A week later Mayor Champetier, who had gone to Avignon for a Socialist congress, caught sight of *la petite* on the back of a motorcycle as it roared along the ramparts, with her arms wrapped around Sterrit's waist, her yellow hair streaming out behind.

Mme. Champetier told her husband to keep his mouth shut. She made up a pot of *oulade* while the men were away in the vineyards and left it at Jean-Baptiste's garden door. But at the laundry trough her own lips were unsealed by Mme. Casaubon, who had grilled the postmistress and found her unable to confirm the use of her phone booth or the arrival of telegrams.

"Just as I feared," said Mme. Casaubon. "No religion, *voyez-vous*, and it's 'legs in the air' for the first foreigner that comes along."

The men were more tactful. When Jean-Baptiste appeared on the *pétanque* ground, Mayor Champetier proposed that he lead the team in the bowling matches at Saint-Genest. The nomination was unanimously approved and sealed in Pastis at the Mickey Bar. Comrades of the Party took care to mention Jean-Baptiste's fight to modernize Barjaux's street lighting. And Amédée Douarnez proclaimed that to be cuckolded by an Avignonnaise was "in the nature of things."

Eulalie echoed her husband's dictum after Mass on Sunday. She added, in a deafening sotto voce, that if M. Cabrillac would accept, she could make him a philter that would render him irresistible to any woman.

Amédée relayed this offer to Jean-Baptiste as they went down the hill together toward the supper hour. Amédée was trundling his wheelbarrow, filled with weeds from the Mayor's garden, along the rim of the village steps. The peasants were coaxing their goats up from the fields. In her dilapidated pergola, Eulalie was cleaning copper pots, blackened with noisome potions. Jean-Baptiste leaned on the fence and, while Amédée grinned, invited her loudly to keep her philters to herself. "I need help from no one."

"And you're not like to get much, Jean-Baptiste Cabrillac," Eulalie shrilled, brandishing a wooden spoon like a wand. "Not from the Comrades anyway." And for all within earshot she added, "Only the old-timers know what to do with the foreigners."

The returns of Clifford Sterrit and Catherine Cabrillac ten days later were separate and unannounced.

Sterrit's motorcycle roared into the yard of the Mickey Bar at the hour of the evening apéritif. He peered through the beaded portiere and, finding that Jean-Baptiste was absent, he slouched in, with his hands in the pockets of his padded jacket. The bartender looked straight at him and then looked away as though he had seen him at the far end of a road. No one having invited him to drink, he gulped down a beer, belched loudly, and went out again.

The next afternoon Catherine got off the bus from Avignon, with her canvas bag slung over her shoulder. Her nose was peeling; her

sun-bleached hair hung in strings around the shoulders of her
T-shirt. She marched straight down the village steps, hardly pausing
at the Cabrillac house, whose shutters were closed. In the sun before
the shepherd's hut, she found Mlle. Pillsbury, standing alone before
a weather-beaten table, lining up baskets and penciling notes on
yellow paper.

Mlle. Pillsbury's blue eyes showed no light. "So here you are," she
said in flat, husky tones, "all ready for work, I don't doubt. You
don't happen to know where Clifford Sterrit might be?"

"I am unable to tell you, Mademoiselle."

"Mme. Casaubon tells me he came back last night. Alone."

Catherine flushed and stared at the baskets. "I see you need
help."

A few well-chosen epithets—*poufiasse, pute, jambes-en-l'air*—
rose from Eugenia Pillsbury's store of dated slang; at the sight of
Catherine's drooping mouth, they died on her lips. "Hadn't you
better go home and get some rest? There is a lot to do, but one more
day won't matter."

Catherine's words came all in a rush. "You need not worry that I
shall cause trouble with M. Sterrit. All that is finished. I thought I
had fallen in love. I was wrong." Once again her clarity cut like a
knife. "I'd be happier," she added, her lip trembling, "if you
would tell M. Sterrit to work only in the caverns from now on, and
not in the hut."

Eugenia Pillsbury found this airy suggestion irritating. Sterrit had
behaved like the slob he was, but he was a good archaeologist, and
she was not his chaperone. "We have work to do," she said. "Lots of
it. And Cliff Sterrit will do it wherever I think best. Keeping the men
at bay is your lookout. But let a neurotic old maid give you one piece
of advice."

Catherine tossed back her lank hair. "What advice is that?"

"You had better watch out, *ma chère*. Someday M. Cabrillac will
blow your pretty head off with that gun of his." The ridges around
Mlle. Pillsbury's mouth were mauve, like the plowed fields of
autumn. "In that case, I'd have to find a new secretary for the dig. It
would be a considerable inconvenience."

Catherine swallowed her anger. She took a deep breath and sought for reassurance in the familiar smells of autumn fruit and burning brush.

Passing back up the steps, she heard a faint creaking of Eulalie Douarnez's gate; her eye caught an even fainter movement of Mme. Casaubon's lace curtain. She did not look back.

On the terrace the basset pattered forward, wagging his long tail. The geraniums needed water. Catherine tried the door. It was open, and she sighed with relief at the coolness of the great dim kitchen.

At first she thought no one was there, but as her eyes adjusted, she saw Jean-Baptiste, sitting like a statue on the bench near the stairs, with his chin in his hands. She gave a little scream and raised her hand to her mouth. Smiling faintly, Jean-Baptiste got up and came toward her. Gently, as though undressing a child, he lifted her bag from her shoulders and pushed back her hair. But when she stretched her arms toward him, he raised his right hand and gave her a blow across the mouth with the back, and another across the cheek with the palm, that sent her spinning into the corner.

When she got up, he repeated this treatment, coldly, without malevolence. Catherine sank to her knees by the hearth, wrapping her arms around her head. When she finally looked up, Jean-Baptiste stood by the door, breathing with little shudders, as if struggling to pass the stone of his own anguish. Catherine understood then that until he passed it, her beating would find no sequel.

She got up with her head in a whirl and made for the stairs.

Hearing overhead the light footstep he had missed for so long, Jean-Baptiste took his shotgun from its rack and went out. The sun had already passed beyond the hobnailed steeple, and the shadows of the houses lengthened across the village steps. As he passed the Douarnez house, Jean-Baptiste raised his hand and found that his fur hat was missing. Then he realized that he was not going to the moors.

The big bed creaked as Catherine stirred from the sprawl in which sleep had seized her. It was getting dark; the air was chilly. Her body ached; her neck was stiff from the blows she had taken.

From the stairway she heard stumbling feet and a low-pitched babbling. She sat up in terror.

Jean-Baptiste swayed in the doorway, his disordered curls lighted by a last ray of sun from the dormer. He was muttering her name, and when she saw the shotgun swinging crazily from his hand, Catherine started to edge her way slowly toward the side of the bed. But he dropped the gun with a clatter and threw himself across the bed, writhing and stretching out his arms. Through the clotted raving of his delirium, she traced the outlines of what had happened.

She got up and leaned over him, cupping his face in her hands. "Hold your tongue, for God's sake."

He sat up then, with his head between his knees, raking his fingers across his skull, as though he might restore his shaken brain through the roots of his hair. Catherine saw him in handcuffs, driven away in the blue truck of the *gendarmerie* to ordeals she could hardly imagine. She pulled his head up again and forced him to look at her.

"We must take the gun downstairs."

He got up and took the gun from the floor, as if he had been a child ordered to pick up a toy. When Catherine lighted the kerosene lamp, she saw gummy streaks on the stock. Jean-Baptiste's hands and cuffs were smeared with reddish brown.

"You must wash yourself. But do not go out to the pump. Stay in the kitchen. I will bring water."

She picked up the lamp and he followed her downstairs. When she came back from the pump, he was sitting on a stool by the chimney, stripped to his drawers. She helped him to wash, wondering at the waxy whiteness of his breast below the seamed tan of his neck, and the narrow fell of hair that ran from throat to navel.

Catherine touched off the fire, and when the blaze had steadied, she sprinkled his shirt with kerosene and stuffed it at the back of the logs. She wiped the stock of the gun with a rag that she threw into the fire. Jean-Baptiste opened the breach; together they picked up the fragments of brass and cardboard that fell on the floor. "These we must bury," she said. "You are sure no one has seen you with the gun?"

"No one." And he added, with a shiver, "I closed his eyes."

Jean-Baptiste pulled on fresh clothes and began oiling and reloading the gun. With the nightfall, the wind had stopped whistling in the eaves; they could hear the bleating of goats and the hollow clanking of their bells. Suddenly there was a thumping, as of something hauled slowly up from step to step. The watchdogs bayed in chorus.

Jean-Baptiste started up. "Amédée's wheelbarrow." He reached for the brandy bottle on the dresser.

Catherine shook her head violently. "You need a clear head. So do I. We must work fast."

He put down the bottle and sat backward on a chair with his arms over the top. Catherine rehearsed him, repeating and listening, over and over, until he shouted with vexation. When he was nearly letter-perfect, she warmed some soup and laid out mountain ham and bread. They ate in silence, Jean-Baptiste wolfing his food. Just as she rose to clear the table, they heard a cascade of voices at their gate. Heavy feet crossed the terrace; a heavy fist struck the door. The basset growled softly.

A high, shallow voice: *"Gendarmerie d'Avignon. Ouvrez!"*

"I'm coming!" She snatched up a plate and went to the door.

Three gendarmes in blue-crowned caps, one with the silver lace of a brigadier, peered in at the girl wiping a plate and the man seated at the table with an apple in his hand. Their florid faces bore the uneasy glaze of duty among strangers.

The Brigadier touched his cap. "Cabrillac, Jean-Baptiste?"

Jean-Baptiste got up slowly. *"C'est moi."*

"Madame, monsieur, a man has been—has been killed. An American of the name"—he consulted a dog-eared notebook—"Sterrit, Clifford. They tell us that your wife—"

"I work for the head of the archaeologists," Catherine said quickly. "For Mlle. Pillsbury. But of course I know M. Sterrit."

The firelight glinted on the Brigadier's buttons. "You will be good enough to come with us then. Both of you. To the Mairie."

"Of course." Catherine frowned at Jean-Baptiste.

"Of course," he echoed. He forced his eyes away from the second gendarme, who was examining the breach of the shotgun. He handed it to the Brigadier, who hefted it for a minute, and then shrugged and put it back on its rack.

Catherine turned down the lamp and set it on the window ledge. She put on her shawl and they all went out and across the terrace, the gendarmes bringing up the rear.

At the Mairie, Amédée Douarnez's wheelbarrow, lined with gunny sacks, was parked near the door. They passed through the echoing *salle des fêtes*, where M. Champetier had married them, and into a back room, where official notices were posted behind chicken wire. Other villagers had begun to arrive through the side door.

Sterrit had been laid out on a trestle, with an army blanket over him. His laced boots stuck up stiffly. The tip of one ear showed; it was blackened with gunpowder. Whenever the door opened, a green-shaded bulb swung gently from the ceiling, and Sterrit's shadow stretched and retracted on the trestle as though he still breathed.

Jean-Baptiste stood pressing his fingers against his eyelids until sparklers flashed silver across the red darkness. Catherine nudged him and he opened his eyes. In the corner, he heard Eulalie Douarnez's drone, punctuated by the staccato of the Brigadier. Yes, oh yes, she had heard something: a commotion down below near the river. She was alone in her kitchen, cutting eggplants and peppers for a *ratatouille*. The Brigadier sighed. "And then I heard shouting and an explosion—maybe there were two—but far away, you know. After a while something went by the house, going up the village steps."

"And what did you do then, madame?"

"Nothing."

"Nothing?"

"Not at first. I thought someone might have come from the moor. Maybe he was having a last go at a rabbit."

"Please, madame. Enough of eggplants and rabbits. Proceed."

Eulalie looked at him with disdain. "Well, finally I did go down, just to make sure. There was no one. Only the goat of Mme. Champetier, munching in the bushes. The black-and-tan, you know. Mlle. Pillsbury had already left." At this juxtaposition the other villagers snickered. "And then"—Eulalie flapped a puffy hand—"and then I saw."

"Saw what, madame?"

"Why, the victim of course. The American. Lying in front of the hut."

"And was the victim still alive?"

"Alive! But monsieur, how could he be alive? His face was like a cheese grater: hundreds of holes. But red. His eyes were closed, but his mouth—well, I have seen many dead, but never such terror. One of his ears—"

"Enough, madame, enough. Tell us now, had M. Sterrit enemies in Barjaux?"

Eulalie's eyes flickered. "But you know how it is with the *Amerloques*: their Indians, their gangsters."

"Madame, I remind you that a man has been killed. Here, in your village, not in Chicago. Now those footsteps going past your house— was it a man or a woman?"

"But monsieur, I saw nothing."

"You *heard*, madame. But what? Slippers? Boots?"

The whole room was silent. Eulalie's chopfallen mouth drew inward; her face puckered till it had no more expression than a prune. There was greater magic in her tongue than in a hundred philters. Her eyes glinted at Jean-Baptiste, and she took a deep breath, swaying on her swollen legs.

"They were the footsteps of Satan, monsieur. But I saw no one."

"*Nom de dieu!*" The Brigadier waved Eulalie away. "Enough, enough!" He looked at the hollow-eyed faces under the swinging lamp, and his glance fell on Catherine. "Madame, be good enough to tell us what you know of these—of these events."

Catherine's voice was low but clear; her calm was also a humility. "Today I rested after my trip. Then I unpacked and set the house to rights."

"You have been away, madame?"

"Yes, for a few days." She picked her way carefully now, looking around for dissent, but no one stirred, not even Mme. Casaubon, who stood in a corner with downcast eyes. "I have been in Avignon. I am an Avignonnaise—originally, but no more—and I have friends there."

"I see. And how well did you know the dead man?"

"M. Sterrit? But very well. We worked together every day."

The Brigadier hesitated. "And how is it that you have not seen him today?"

"As I have told you, I stayed at home today." Catherine's voice strengthened. "My husband came home early. I made supper and we ate together, as you know."

"Did your husband take his shotgun from the house today?"

Catherine pulled her shawl around her. "That you must ask him, *M. le Brigadier*. I do not follow him about. But this I can tell you: he takes the shotgun only to the moor. Today he did not go to the moor. *Et voilà*."

Jean-Baptiste answered the Brigadier's questions with long pauses. The villagers were used to that; it was one of the qualities they liked best. Little by little they had pressed in closer around him and Catherine. And now M. Champetier raised his voice, straining his words through snaggle teeth: "I am not of M. Cabrillac's Party, but I can tell you he has always put the welfare of Barjaux first. The Americans—well, their digging may bring us fame. But often they are careless. About other people, I mean; and not only in Barjaux." He looked around the room, and then at the body on the trestle. "Who can say where M. Sterrit may have made enemies? He is dead and cannot tell us. And we must say no more."

Mme. Champetier said shyly that she had known Jean-Baptiste from boyhood: "A good and patient man."

The Brigadier referred to his notebook and turned again to Jean-Baptiste. "Members of your Party are not known for their love of the Americans. But you bore no grudge against them, no rancor against the victim?"

Jean-Baptiste flushed. "My grudges are not important. Everyone knows my feelings about strangers in Barjaux." He looked squarely at the Brigadier. "Any strangers. But they will not be here forever."

"And your wife?"

"My wife feels as we all do."

Mme. Casaubon raised her eyebrows, but the others nodded and murmured. The Brigadier looked at his colleagues: a screen of fire was mounting between them and the villagers. The case was clear, but where were the witnesses? And with a shotgun—what evidence? He gave a curt command, and the third gendarme jerked the blanket down from Sterrit's head. Jean-Baptiste did not flinch. The eyelids were still shut; the pitted face had been washed; the shattered jaw bound up in a towel. It was the head of a doll; nothing of Sterrit was left on the trestle—or anywhere. Jean-Baptiste glanced around at all the eyes, fixed on him in the harsh light, and his fears melted.

The Brigadier said loudly that the principal witnesses would remain available. M. Champetier, with the shadow of a smile, promised the continued cooperation of the village. The Brigadier brushed imaginary dust from his lapel, and his medals danced. He threw open the side door that led to the parvis. Stars glittered above the steeple; the wind was rising.

"Mistral," said Mme. Champetier. "Clear weather tomorrow."

"And good health," said Eulalie Douarnez.

When the gendarmes had gone, the Mayor covered Sterrit's face. Mme. Champetier brought candles from the *salle des fêtes* and switched off the bulb. Then she went out to fetch coffee for those who had volunteered to watch with the body.

Halfway down the steps, Catherine and Jean-Baptiste met Mlle. Pillsbury. She peered at them in the dimness. "Will you be with us in the morning, madame?"

"You have not heard the news then?" Catherine asked breath-
lessly.

"I've heard nothing else. I'm on my way to see the Mayor."

"Ah?"

Mlle. Pillsbury tweaked the brim of her felt hat. "You have nothing to fear from me, my dear. I only want to get on with the work. I
know what I know, but I'll leave the guessing to others."

"You are going ahead with the next cavern?" asked Jean-Baptiste.

Mlle. Pillsbury's calm was monumental. "We must finish before
the end of the month. I doubt that any of us will be anxious to come
back next year."

"My wife will not be there tomorrow, mademoiselle."

"I was afraid you would say that. Well, we shall miss her."

"I have not forgotten your little boxes," said Jean-Baptiste. "You
shall have them by next week."

"Splendid," said Mlle. Pillsbury. "Good-bye now."

To his relief, she did not offer her hand.

Catherine hurried ahead toward where the lamp beckoned, like a
breathing presence, from their window. So she would go no more to
the domed hut. No more scratching pencils, no more clacking typewriter. No alien hands to touch her, no easeful laughter to echo in
her ears, nor even the gravelly voice of Mlle. Pillsbury, speaking of
things that lay on the far side of time. And soon would come the
long, wet silences of winter. Suddenly she felt a throb of wild regret,
like a surge of pain in the gut. She stumbled on the terrace steps, but
when Jean-Baptiste's hand gripped her elbow, it was finished.

In the dark attic, Catherine dropped her clothes in a pool at her
feet. She slipped her nightgown over her head and wiggled in between the lavender-smelling sheets. Then she fell into sleep as
though into a well.

In the kitchen, Jean-Baptiste banked the embers, from which a
thread of smoke drifted upward. He opened the door for the basset
and stood watching the stars wheeling across the southern sky. Far
away he heard the whisper of the river.

His fingers moved but made no sign.

The lamp cast long shadows on the stairs and among the attic rafters. And as he held it nearer to Catherine's face, she muttered in her sleep. He watched her faint breathing, and his body stirred. Blowing out the lamp, he stripped and slid in beside her. His hand touched her breast under the coarse nightgown. She did not turn, but drew up her knees so that her little rump fitted into the hollow of his belly. In the night she would waken: or in the morning—what did it matter? He knew, as he staggered downward to join her inside the gates of sleep, that nothing could destroy what lay between them now.

The Furies

... Facies non omnibus una
Nec diversa tamen, qualem decet esse sororum
—Ovid

After Hugh Orton had guided his wife and sister-in-law down the gangplank and through the cement labyrinth that surrounded the customs shed, he called a momentary halt. He waited there in the sun, with the women fidgeting behind him, while his memories of the tiered city that lay before them withered and fell. Gone were the stretches of sand and surf, the glistening undulation of tiled roofs, the line of white villas on the hill. In their place were office buildings, thrusting up like teeth in a broken comb; smutted stucco, brown palm fronds; drifts of plastic and paper, whirling aimlessly, like the gulls overhead, in the damp breeze.

As they straggled toward the medina, Hugh realized that his trajectory had missed the secret target. He might slope off into one alley or peer furtively into another, but with the two women in tow, he didn't dare search too intensely. Bravo for the nation builders! Their puritanism had cleared away the shaded courtyards of the *bousbir*, the fountains, and the tesselated cribs where the colonials had taken their pleasure. Either that, or the arcades and the little windows with their blue and red panes had succumbed to some ruthless urban amputation, whose scars were powdered over by the siftings of neglect.

What portion, he wondered, had the masters of the new order reserved for Aicha? And the black Mauritanian, with her gold teeth and shining breasts? The turbaned *goumiers*, with their hawk noses and their cartridge belts?

"If you *must* keep dashing off like that," said Theresa, "we'll simply never get back to the ship in time for lunch. We seem to spend half our time on this dratted cruise traipsing up and down the native quarters."

"Isn't that the main idea?" Hugh asked. The mole at the corner of his eye was obstructing his view more and more these days; he turned full face now toward his wife. "I thought this stop would be a bit special, after all. But I suppose you don't care about going back to the old consulate."

"My dear Hugh, after ten years of retirement, who do you think is going to remember either of us? They won't remember me anyway, that's for sure."

Marjorie gave a playful whinny. "Maybe Hugh would be happier if we just left him to wander around on his own."

Hugh turned sharply. But in his sister-in-law's widened green eyes he could see nothing special, nothing beyond her customary slyness.

At the edge of the souk he recognized the faded blue shutters of Berrada's Bazaar. Could the three of them find common ground, he wondered, among the carpets and brass and gilded leather?

"You know what I think of these places," Theresa whispered. "Even in the old days, there was nothing worth all that haggling." She splayed her gloved fingers at him (gloves always in native quarters; that was the rule) as he pushed open the lattice. "And now that they've got their independence"—the four syllables were eloquent of her scorn—"well, you'd do better to whistle up a pickpocket and hand over your money right away."

"But Tessie," Marjorie pleaded, "it looks fascinating. Right out of the *Arabian Nights*. You never know: we may turn up simply treasures, my dear!"

Children and widowhood had made Marjorie less angular than her sister, who hadn't been blessed with either. But her antiphonies harmonized admirably—almost comically during the cruise—with his wife's muffled grievances. Here, as in other ports of call, her gushing and clasping of hands only brightened the flame of disapproval that burned behind Theresa's pearl-studded glasses. Even their hair—Marjorie's tinted auburn; Theresa's assisted gold—was coiled similarly under sensible confections of denim. And as their moon-pale faces, strangers to the African sun, hovered over the spoils of the bazaar, the two of them sucked away the very marrow of adventure.

Hassan Berrada floated in the middle distance, watching, as he always had, for the lighted eye, the tender handling of tray or vase, that signaled the moment to pounce. Djellaba and burnoose conspired to blur the outlines of decay: a sprouting of white hair at the edge of draped linen, an insinuation of paunch under the strip of embroidered buttonholes. The years had passed lightly over Hassan.

And the years had produced a new presence. Near the back wall a young man sat cross-legged, drinking tea. His brown forearm, from which he had rolled back his full sleeve, moved rhythmically against the parti-colored geometry of a Berber rug as he raised and lowered the steaming glass.

The comforting pungency of mint: Hugh remembered now the dented silver pot, the saucer sticky with sugar, on Aicha's bedside table. He saw again the long, shining hair on the bolster, the coarse sheets in disarray, the faint blue tattoos between closed eyes, the nipples hardening under his fingers, darkening in the blood-red light. All that twining and thrashing and fierce, oblivious thrusting during the long evenings—could they really have produced nothing? No tomorrow there either? No one to confront the changing world, like this dusky apparition by the wall, so straight and somber in the gleaming envelope of youth, with the cap of black curls beneath his fez.

"Tessie," he asked, "what ever happened to the big silver box we bought here?"

"Silver box?" Her black-leathered fingers tapped her chin. "I don't remember any silver box."

"It was more like pewter really. No ornaments at all. Berber, not Arab." The wings of his insistence began to fan other memories. "I kept papers and old photos in it."

"Oh, that! But it was brass, Hugh, plated brass. You stuffed it so full that the hinges simply fell apart. I put it away somewhere when we transferred to Holland. Artsy-craftsy: those things just don't hold up."

The papers and photos hadn't held up either. They couldn't quite flesh out the memoirs he had dreamed of: plump and suave they should have been, and sprinkled with the candied fruit of anecdote. ("I told Ahram Pasha he was talking nonsense. After some hesitation he drew me into the hall and admitted that at the Residency they were already burning files. . . . ") Group photos of notables, of course, with Consul General Hugh Orton not too far off camera. And the frontispiece: double-breasted pinstripe; handkerchief peeping from pocket; flat wet hair: wise diplomat of yesteryear, who had predicted the collapse of the Protectorate and saved the American missionaries from mutilation and massacre by fanatics. The first edition would have been bound in ribbed leather; if you held the thick pages to the light, a winged watermark sprang into view.

Hugh closed his eyes: through the vellum he recaptured an afternoon of a long-lost summer.

A tiny airdrome in the mountains, with snow still powdering the peaks and the concrete strip shimmering in the heat. Through the windows of the shed, a flash of green and gold where barley rippled at the edge of the desert. On the opposite side, wave on wave of red rock dropping to the far-off glitter of the sea.

The Commandant was still away, making the rounds of his mountain domain. Already the gnat of a monoplane that had brought Hugh up from the coast was being wheeled out of its toy-town hangar for the return. If he missed it, he would have to telegraph back to the consulate and then spend the night at the *gîte d' étape.* In the early morning there was a bus; the prospect of lurching down through the passes in the pink dawn, with Berber tribesmen in striped robes, and bicycles and squawking chickens on the roof, was not unpleasant. It would fortify him for the eyes of Theresa when he got to the villa a day late.

No matter the delay: he couldn't leave without settling the status of the missionaries. Diplomatic notes were no remedy for zealots: he had to confront the Commandant face to face.

At last the descending snarl of a single engine brought the station to life. Burnoosed heads glided past the windows like targets in a penny arcade. The flies near the ceiling revved up their drowsy circling. The Commandant, in short-sleeved blouse and kepi, with gold bars on his shoulders, stepped gingerly across the tarmac, as though on hot coals. Two turbaned *goumiers* capered in his wake, and when he reached the door, there was a general hush and a chaos of salutes.

From the correspondence Hugh had expected a younger man, not this ramrod, with thick graying hair and sharp-lidded eyes, and the authority of power effectually wielded. His glance took in the alien presence by the window; he beckoned to one of the sergeants, who whispered in his ear. A start of surprise, and the Commandant crossed over to shake hands. He motioned toward the hallway. "I will lead the way, *Monsieur le Consul.*"

In the freight office that also served as audience chamber there were straw-wrapped bundles of dates, cases of oranges, and a huge table, encrusted with nacre and piled with blue dossiers. Behind these the Commandant positioned his chair. He waved Hugh to a hemp-bottomed armchair and shoved a tin of black cigarettes at him. "Sorry you had to wait. You were expected, but no one thought to tell me before I left yesterday. What can I do for you, *Monsieur le Consul?*"

At the mention of the missionaries, the Commandant's face clouded. "I have heard much of them during my trip. Too much. Two of them behave well: no fuss. The other two cause talk. In the hills talk means trouble. And in the *Affaires Indigènes* we have trouble enough already."

"What kind of trouble? Perhaps we can help."

"The second two have begun to pray in public and to hold meetings. They belong to one of your curious sects—something to do with baptism."

Hugh smiled. "They're non-Convention Baptists. The quiet pair are old-fashioned Methodists."

"*Mon dieu!*" The Commandant raised his hands in mock horror. "But never mind which heresy they profess. At their dispensary the Baptists proselytize among the Moslems. The treaty, as you know, forbids anything of that sort. It obliges France to protect Islam, and in the mountains Islam is a little special."

"Of course. But I'm told these people do good work."

"No doubt," said the Commandant drily, "at least by their own lights. But I cannot risk further incidents for the sake of canned milk and bandages."

"There have been incidents?"

"Not with your people—not yet. But two of the Moslems who went often to the Benedictines at Zarou were found wandering on the edge of the oasis with the mutilations reserved for those who speak evil."

"What is that?"

The Commandant folded and unfolded his thin fingers on the table. "Their tongues had been cut down to the root. That punishment is not uncommon in this country."

"You've told the American missionaries?"

"Oh yes. But it only redoubles their zeal. I would like to expel them all before we have more tongues cut."

"Expelling them would cause complications." Hugh took care to hold down the tone. "I suppose they feel the Lord leaves them no choice. But I'll ask Washington to intervene with the parent churches. It has to be handled gently: a touchy subject back home, you know. I'll ask the two Baptists to stop in at the consulate."

"Bravo! Much better for them to come to you, away from their parishioners. Tell them to stick to good works and we won't object; they can even whisper a bit when they hand out toothbrushes."

"As long as they keep within bounds, we count on you to protect them. The treaty goes into that too."

"Oh, I'm quite aware of it. The missionaries never let me forget it." He added with a groan and a wink, "Yours are not the only ones. The universal churches never hesitate to appeal to the nation-state. Will you take a beer?"

"I'd like a beer. But I mustn't miss the plane."

"I'll have them hold it a few minutes. I think there are no other passengers, and it will be light for hours." He wiped his forehead and lifted the phone from its long-necked stand. "I'm sure the pilot will be thirsty too."

"In that case, with pleasure."

The Commandant barked briefly into the phone. Then he leaned back, abandoning the von Stroheim posture, and unbuttoned his collar. An Arab in white jacket and fez bustled in with two beaded tankards on a brass tray.

2

As Marjorie grappled clangorously with the brass trays, the young man at the back of the shop rose suddenly from his knees. Pushing the tea stand aside with slippered foot, he advanced across the carpets. Hugh could see that the profile was Hassan's, but sharper, more elegant, as though some martial strain had worked its way back up, through generations of shopkeepers.

"May I help you?" His voice was unexpectedly treble, yet even and soothing. "Something to please the ladies? We have fine leather too, you know."

Blank looks between the sisters. They turned simultaneously, arms upraised, like automatons on a town clock. Hugh imagined them striking him in alternation: hammer blow from Theresa, coy tap from Marjorie. One stroke for every second of the predicament into which male insouciance had drawn them.

"Tell him we're just looking," Theresa said.

"Yes, yes," Marjorie panted. "And let's hear a little of your famous Arabic."

This time he accepted her gambit. *"Saha,"* he began hoarsely. *"Ghadi nekhamman' alyeh:* we must decide later."

The young man's jaw dropped. With a swiveling shake of his head that verged on complicity, he excluded the women from the circuit. He glanced at his father, but Hassan, standing watchful in his corner, only smiled and did not stir.

"Mezziane, very good," said the youth ironically. His right hand fanned out across his chest. On the middle finger, Hugh noticed a silver band, with a murderous point on the bezel. *"Allah i' aref."*

"Allah i' aref."

The young man glided toward the back of the shop. He looked around once, and his tongue, darting like a lizard's, flicked a crumb of sugar from his lip. Then he lifted a clicking bead portiere and was gone in a flash of white.

"Gracious!" Marjorie giggled. "What a gorgeous creature! Like a ghost. And that wicked-looking ring. What was all that about Allah?"

"Oh, Allah comes in everywhere. When I said we'd decide later, he reminded me that it's really Allah who makes the decisions. A useful formula; the young man was embarrassed."

Theresa snorted. *"He* should be embarrassed!"

"Natural enough, Tessie." Hugh warmed; he felt almost paternal. "He was trying out his father's sales tactics, but he jumped his cue a bit, that's all."

Hassan moved into the breach; with a bow, he held out two stud boxes of pink leather. "Just the thing for your boys," Hugh told Marjorie. Ignoring Theresa's mutterings, he drew out his wallet.

Recognition flickered between him and Hassan; he would have liked to compliment him on his son. But he shrank from blowing on embers that were nearly extinguished. Their eyes flickered and turned aside, as though some passage of lust or treachery lay half-buried between them, and while the bargaining ritual followed its course, Hugh's vision unfolded again.

The Commandant refilled Hugh's tankard. "I knew your people well during the landings," he said. "Especially the wartime Consul—but right now his name escapes me."

"Wilcox."

"No, before that."

"O'Brien."

"That's it. He was something more than a consul, I think."

"One of my oldest friends." Hugh took a long draft of the cold beer. "Yes, he was more than a consul; in those days consuls had special jobs to do, and we needed people with special skills."

"Very clever, O'Brien. And always a member of the team." He looked hopefully at Hugh, the new boy. "He was very attached to these *montagnards*. Like me. He always said they would be the last to desert us."

"To desert you?"

"You are surprised? But the handwriting is already clear. There are the anti-colonials in Cairo and New York—and in your own government. Our military is an embarrassment to Paris, and even to the civilians in the Residency down here. We shan't be here much longer."

"I suppose it's inevitable. But I hate to think what will happen when you leave."

"Thank you, *Monsieur le Consul*." The Commandant was silent for a minute. Then he said, "You are quite right: it will not be pretty. You know the last time I was at the Residency, some young prig in the Diplomatic Cabinet had the nerve to tell me that we must take care in the *Affaires Indigènes* to avoid the imputation of fascism."

"Good God!"

"Yes, good God. So I told him what happened five years ago at Ain-El-Horm. Mountaineers from another tribe killed every living thing: children, hospital patients, cattle, chickens; they even pulled up the blades of grass in the caid's garden. All for some absurd rumor about a plan to divert their water to the town. Fascism, communism—what the hell!"

"One of our *chaouches* is a mountaineer," Hugh said. "I'm told they're splendid people, but when they're agitated by the unknown, they become maniacs. Like anyone, I suppose."

"A mere spark will set them off. Your friends in the hills should understand that."

"No friends of mine, *mon Commandant*. Nor even coreligionists. So that makes me all the more responsible for them."

"Compatriots then; misguided—like mine. But compatriots all the same."

"Exactly."

So they drained their glasses in understanding. Dizzy from strong beer and the heat, Hugh was escorted to the little plane and packed off in style, with salutes all around.

Exhilaration carried him through the short, rough flight—it was rather like being shaken in a paper bag—and when they landed, instead of phoning the consulate for his car, he took a taxi straight to the Reserved Quarter.

3

At the end of the boulevard that led from the medina towered the aseptic bulk of the cruise ship, an alien water bird enmeshed in cables and rings. Theresa pushed ahead, rather like a ship herself, with scarf ends flying and her two tugboats puffing alongside. The gulls whirled overhead, screaming their warnings of disaster.

"I don't like the look of that business near your eye," Theresa said, as they paused at the foot of the gangplank. "Why not let the ship's doctor have a look?"

"Ah, those epidermis things. You never know," Marjorie chanted, "you just never know. But of course skin cancers aren't *always* serious, are they?"

The coils of her hair glistened like serpents in the sunlight. Secret stings for secret sins, Hugh thought. And he remembered Hassan's son. *"Allah i' aref,"* he said.

At the top of the gangplank he took a deep breath. "I'm going ashore again. There are still old spots I want to see before we sail tonight. You girls can stretch out in comfort."

"You're going without lunch?" Theresa asked. But tourist fatigue had drained her of wifely concern.

Hugh turned and scuttled down the gangplank. At the bottom, yielding to dimly remembered superstition, he skipped the last rubber square and landed on the concrete with both feet. When he looked up, the sisters had vanished. Even the gulls had melted away in the noonday void. On the mast of the ship, a red-and-black pennant snapped suddenly in the wind.

As he retraced the morning's path, his eyelid began to flutter with a life of its own. Just as he raised a finger to still it, he saw the passageway. Like everything revisited, it had shrunk: a mere crevice now in the haphazard of concrete. At the end he found the three little houses, clustered around the tiled fountain, and the arched windows. But the fountain had gone dry. The silence was unbroken by the whine of Arab music. And no lamps would ever glow again, red and blue behind the windowpanes, with the promise of hide-and-seek in the dark corners of body and soul.

Nothing interrupted the hum of the vast medina that encircled the courtyard. Hugh sank down on the familiar steps and buried his face in his hands. Once again the winged watermark glowed behind his eyelids.

By the time he got from the airport to the Reserved Quarter, twilight had come down. He paid off his taxi and went first to the bar, which was beginning to resound with the thump of army boots and the reedy music of the gramophone.

Aicha was nowhere in sight. And when he climbed the stairs, he found the little room empty, the bed stripped down, the table bare. In the hall the black giantess from Mauritania who shared the crib told him in pidgin French, with uneasy flashes of gold teeth, that Aicha had been moved to another part of the *bousbir*. The Mauritanian's smile faded when he tried to hem her in. "She say you not come there. Police too: they say no for you."

His visits had been watched then; officialdom had been unofficially disquieted. The Consul had been foolish: he had shown himself too often; always he had gone to the same girl. With the swift unraveling of the colonial fabric, Moroccan attachments to outsiders no doubt touched the nerves of the police. Who could say where the nationalist flame burned brightest or how it was fed? And if the Arabs had mutilated one another and murdered the Senegalese soldiers in the Quarter, why not the Americans? One thing was clear now: the Residency wanted no riddles about consuls—their secrets, their disappearance—to haunt its files. He stood for a moment in the darkening hall, stiff with hatred for the prudent hands that had reached down to save him. In a twinkling they had snuffed out the bull's-eye lantern that had lighted him at last, in his third decade, to the knowledge of death that lay at the frontiers of the flesh.

And what about the missionaries and their converts? Had he and the Commandant exacted the same price for their safety? Once orders had been enforced on you, the walls of your labyrinth vanished: the path lay flat and straight; no mystery drew you further on to bliss or to destruction.

Hugh thrust a banknote into the hand of the Mauritanian, who gaped at the denomination. *"Pour elle,"* he said, *"pour Aicha."* She looked thoughtful, but he put his faith in her solidarity. And if the money never got to Aicha, did it really matter any more?

Back at the villa, Theresa had already gone to her room. She did not stir when he looked in, but at breakfast, the hour of his return was noted.

"I do worry about you, Hugh. I have no way of knowing where you are. Not that it matters any more."

How could he ever tell her what had been gained and lost in an afternoon? "Let's just say that it was a long day, Tessie."

After that he went no more to the *bousbir*, but he hugged even more closely to himself the secrets his wife's eyes had discerned but never pierced.

4

Hugh stirred on the cold tiles. Again his eyelid fluttered, and he flicked angrily at the mole with his thumb. A blinding gush of blood. Voices and footsteps in the passage swelled with his pain and then receded into the gabble and buzz of the medina beyond. But as he struggled to clear the crimson web that wavered and spread before his eyes, he found that he was no longer alone.

A lithe arm entwined his waist like a wire and gently, tentatively, raised him to his feet. Fingers traveled down his back in a caress, half-filial, half-sexual. Images floated up through his confusion: official seals and gold wafers, gold epaulettes, dark loosened hair, and then the silver box, half-opened on a disorder of letters and photos.

Suddenly he felt metal pressing against his thigh, probing insistently. The ring with the stiletto point: Berrada's son? But why here?

As his samaritan drew him closer, Hugh smelled spice and oil and sweat. And what had happened to the white djellaba? It was streaked with grime, and stained under the arms. The face that loomed through his blurred vision had aged: the skin had thickened, the eye sockets had darkened.

And when the lips curled back, Hugh made out, behind the broken teeth, a stump of flesh, crisscrossed by a net of sinews, all strung with pearls of spit. Against this bridle, the glistening muscle struggled convulsively but produced only clotted babble.

He wrenched himself from the man's embrace with a harsh cry and dropped at the edge of the fountain. The last thing he heard was the slap of bare feet hurrying across the tiles.

Two of the pasha's police found him on their sunset rounds. They hauled him to his feet, watching sardonically as he scrubbed at the sticky blood on his face. They did not ask for his papers; their gestures told him what they thought: another drunken American, spoiled child of the great ships, looking for adventure in the fabled *bousbir*. "All that finished," they told him smugly. "No more girl. Wrong address. *Fissa*: out—quick!" They set him on his course, like a mechanical toy, snickering as he tottered along the arcades.

When he passed Hassan Berrada's bazaar, the lattices were thrown open to the evening air. A slim, robed figure bent and straightened and bent again, like a peasant among the vines, clearing the litter left by pawing tourists, stacking rugs and cushions for tomorrow's pillage. His dark curls were neatly combed and his djellaba was still snow-white. He stared briefly at Hugh and his eyes widened. Then he turned away.

Halfway to the port, Hugh stopped under a palm tree to wipe his eye and stow his bloody handkerchief. When he groped in his hip pocket, he found the lining cut away: wallet and passport were gone. He was beyond surprise, beyond anything but a flicker of amusement: how many times had he extricated others from this fix?

The sun was dropping fast behind the ship; the dark edges of the violet sky presaged a stormy passage. Overhead, long lines of gulls streamed back from the sea, sobbing and shrieking at the unfathomable deception that had moved them to flight. One of them lighted on a piling; when its wings were folded, the creature had the paunch and pipestem legs, the round resentful eye, of an old man. It flapped off to join the others, and Hugh pushed on, girding himself against the assault—would this one be the last?—that awaited him whenever he found strength to mount the gangplank.

The Visa

Squeezing himself and his bags through the revolving door of the Hotel Kasteel, Tom Calhern pushed his way into the street, only to find that there were no taxis in sight. He had forgotten that the town was celebrating the first anniversary of the Liberation. Bombed-out windows, still gaping at the ruins, were festooned with the Dutch tricolor; on public buildings the royal motif was marked by strings of orange globes that pulsated on rationed electricity in the April dusk. Now and then a bicycle bell tinkled wanly or a jeep roared past, but the pavements were left open to the Rotterdammers, who walked about mechanically, still in the daze of deliverance, waving small flags and raising their voices in tentative song. Less inhibited were the soldiers and sailors, mainly British and Canadian, who formed up in knots, bumping and shoving each other like good-natured hippos, raucously shouting their favorite ballad:

> Roll me over in the clover,
> Roll me over, lay me down
> And do it again.

Liberation Day, Calhern realized, was going to be far from ideal for moving, even for a fledgling vice-consul who had learned from the army to travel light (all his belongings were in his two suitcases) and travel fast. To outlanders—especially if they were "civilian pigs"—the bedraggled city offered inconvenience with no compensating throb of heroic recollection, no sense of relief from ordeals.

He found himself wondering how his own Minneapolis would have adapted itself to catastrophe.

But self-pity was surely not the right note for an American. With his bags bumping about his ankles, Calhern set off toward the Great Canal. He looked back once at the twin towers of the Hotel Kasteel, and at the windows glittering above the expanses of rubble. The exemption of the building from bombs and from the fire that had gutted the surrounding blocks was a favorite target of the Rotterdammers' irony. And the soldiers and officials who guzzled and danced and whored at the Kasteel turned a blind eye to the wreckage that had washed up on the doorstep. A pain in the ass, Calhern had told himself a dozen times; in moving out, he had opted—was he being priggish?—for a closer view, a greater share, of the troubles of Europe. Perhaps he would find reality again at the Pension Rohrabach.

The pension was, in fact, a large apartment overlooking the Great Canal from the fourth floor of a scarred and shaken block of flats. The Rohrabachs rented their extra rooms to prevent the housing autocrats from quartering the military or the dreaded refugees from Indonesia. Vice-Consul Mills, who was also a slave on the visa assembly line, had lived there; when he was transferred to Antwerp, Calhern had snapped up his room, sight unseen.

Panting from his climb (elevators rarely worked these days), Calhern paused before a spotless brass plate marked "Engineer Rohrabach" and rang the bell. The man who immediately flung open the door, as though he had been awaiting his cue, was a burgher of substance: tall, angular, florid, with slanted eyelids and impenetrable pupils like those of a goat. Calhern knew he was about sixty: according to Mills, he had served in the Dutch marines after the First World War, and despite a rounding of paunch, he had kept a heroic carriage. As he escorted his new pensioner, he proved sparing of words—a blessing in officers and consuls, so why not in landlords?

The rooms were laid out on a lavish scale and strewn with loot, colonial and domestic: Javanese pottery, silver bric-a-brac, Delft jars. On the walls hung brown-gravy landscapes in gilt frames; giblets of oriental carpeting trailed over tables and chairs as well as

floors. But no vestiges of opulence could quite efface the chill that
lingered after four winters without fuel.

Calhern's impression that everything had been "laid on" for his
arrival was reenforced by his first glimpse of Mevrouw Rorhrabach,
who was posed as chatelaine in a wing chair before an almost imper-
ceptible fire. She looked at least twenty years younger than the Engineer, and she deployed a voluble and slightly gamy charm,
twisting her rings on pale fingers, fluttering blue-veined eyelids,
patting blue hair, which she wore tightly curled at the ends. In a
pastiche of French and Dutch (her mother, she explained, was a
Walloon), she warbled about the delights of Paris and Brussels and
New York. But her gush did not drown the Belgian zest for bargaining.

While her husband stood by the window, cracking his knuckles,
she opened the bidding briskly. *"Enfin, monsieur,* fifty guilders a
week then. Is that agreeable?"

"Mr. Mills told me thirty-five."

Her eyes narrowed, and she sought firmer ground in Dutch:
"Your friend did not have the best room. And he rarely ate breakfast here."

Calhern happened to know that the second statement was untrue.
And haggling always made him feel like a duffer. "Maybe we could
settle for forty. The hotel was only fifty-five—and with private
bath."

"Ah, private bath!" She shook her blue curls at him, as though he
had affronted the civilization of Erasmus and Vermeer. "No, that
we cannot offer. We have few of the American comforts nowadays."

The Engineer loomed behind the wing chair. "Forty-five if Mr.
Calhern agrees to stay for six months, eh Grietje? Mr. Calhern is an
American official, after all, and we can never repay our debt to the
Americans."

"Bien entendu," his wife fluted. Authority had clearly given her
an elbow in the ribs. "Quite right, my dear."

Calhern's toes curled. His appetite for family life took a sharp
drop. But what the hell: the hotel had probably filled his room
within minutes; retreat was cut off. "Okay then," he said. "Perhaps
I'd better put away my things."

"Let me find Leni." Mrs. Rohrabach got up, smoothing her skirt over her hips; the gesture seemed to erase the rufflings of her temper too. "Leni will help you. She is at your service—as we all are."

Calhern expected to hear that the servant was clean if not clever. And then he remembered there was a daughter. "Not bad either," Mills had told him. "She needs fresh air, poor girl, and development: there's plenty of room for development."

But pity was misplaced: Leni turned out to be anything but a drudge. She followed him into his room like a kid sister, and while he hung his clothes in a gigantic wardrobe, she raced about, flicking at imaginary dust, her breasts joggling under a skimpy white housedress. She had her mother's round face, but her high color was her father's, and probably the straight yellow hair that swung about her shoulders. Her pale eyes didn't waver before Calhern's stare, and she kept up a soft chatter in textbook British English, interspersed with caressing murmurs of "*Als'tublieft*" as she handed him towels or opened drawers.

"Your English is perfect."

"Do you think so? We study it in school. Everyone learns English now, you know."

"Do they?"

"Naturally. Before—I mean up to now, it was German. But that's finished for good." She tweaked at the silk bedspread. "I hope one day to go to your country. Is it very difficult?"

"Right now it's not easy."

"Is it so expensive?"

"It's not that so much. But there are lots of people who want to come now. We haven't got room for everybody." He smiled. "We're not so hospitable as we used to be."

Leni pouted at his irony. "I can't believe that." She glanced around the room. "Everything looks quite okay, don't you think? It is time to drink coffee. We ought not to keep my parents waiting."

On the Friday after his move, Calhern stayed late at the Consulate. Spring had doubled the business of the visa section, and the old brick house in the Parklaan (it had been confiscated from a Dutch Nazi and turned over to the Americans) seemed to be packing in half the Netherlanders, with their tales of woe and their pleas for escape. Calhern wanted to shine at his first post. He wanted to sympathize with those who waited stolidly on the benches in the old drawing room that lay beyond the glass doors of his office. But he had begun to resent the importunate, whose requests covered his desk with mounting piles of blue folders. Tonight he resolved not to leave the building until he had settled the hash of at least half the applicants whose dossiers filled his "pending" box. For nearly an hour he sifted through boasts of wealth and achievement, past and to come, and protestations of political virginity; when at last he looked up, the Consul General was peering in through the glass doors.

Twenty-five years of skeptical games with regulations had hardened the Consul General to the whimpers of immigrants, and Calhern, as he slid open the doors, was shamefully glad to see his lantern jaw and sardonic smile.

"Cheer up, Tom," he said. "They'll live even if you don't get them all past Ellis Island."

"I suppose they will, sir, but I can't separate sheep from goats. After a while they all look alike."

"Some of the goats will get around you. They'll expect you to believe in their virtue, especially if they have any money left. Fortunately most of them are harmless."

"What about the collaborators?"

"Who will they collaborate with in the States? In another five years, when we've spent our moral passions, they'll get in scot-free. Then the communists will have to sweat. And after that maybe the fascists again. But in Holland you're not in much danger of letting a Goebbels or a Lenin slip past you."

"Some of them are pretty notorious, though. Would you give a visa to the owner of this house?"

"Of course not. But that's a question of public relations. Black and white are clearer to the survivors. And to politicians back home, too." He shrugged. "Never mind, Tom; at least you'll get practice saying no. It's not bad training: too many diplomats have been ruined by the desire to please."

Calhern grinned. "I know what you mean. I've just moved in with Mills's Dutch family. I have a feeling they want something too."

"Ah, the Rohrabachs. He's a tough nut, the Engineer. The wife is pretty dreadful, I'm told: a frustrated butterfly. There's a girl too, isn't there?"

"Yes, sir. But it's the parents I wonder about."

"Then I'd say you're not making the best use of your spare time. Why not come along now and have dinner with my wife and me? We can offer you a bourbon—unless you'd rather drown your worries in Dutch gin."

"A bourbon sounds much better."

At the pension the dishes had been cleared long ago, and the three Rohrabachs sat by the fire. Calhern was conscious of a break in their talk when he came in. Leni embroidered; her mother knitted; Mynheer entered figures on yellow paper, tapping his long chin with his pencil.

"So"—Mevrouw pointed a knitting needle roguishly at him—"so you have dined late this night."

"Yes, and worked late too."

"Ah, *le pauvre!* And what keeps you so busy?"

"My wife has not heard," said the Engineer, "of the sudden popularity of your country. But there are others who have, eh?"

Leni looked up from her work. "Of course they've heard of it, Papa. Why wouldn't they?"

"Quite right, my dear. Why not? What's left for them here? First our enemies destroy our cities, and now our friends are relieving us of our colonies."

Calhern ignored this thrust. "Everyone has troubles these days."

The glance that passed between the older Rohrabachs was an exclusion: a child—and a foreigner! What does he know of trouble.

"But surely, it's different in America," Leni said. "There's more of a future, more hope for everybody, no?"

"I guess so. It depends on what you're hoping for."

"We have friends in New York," said Mrs. Rohrabach, with a shiver of complacency. "Very kind—oh, so kind all during the Occupation. Clothes, and then the food packages—even when we didn't need them. The Schermerhorns, on Seventy-second Street. Very wealthy. But perhaps you have heard of them?"

"I'm afraid not."

"Petroleum," said the Engineer.

"*Très gentils,* les Schermerhorn." Mrs. Rohrabach raised her needle like a wand. "*Et très, très riches.*"

The Engineer cracked his knuckles. "They visited us here, Mr. Calhern, before the war and the rebellion in the Indies."

"Ah then," said his wife, "this town was not too bad. And The Hague—well, I remember a dinner there, given for the Schermerhorns by our friends from the Shell Company. There were diplomats, too, and even the Queen's secretary. At the Royal, it was. You know the Royal, I'm sure. But nowadays it is nothing, nothing: boiled fish and carrots. Our cities are quite asleep."

When her parents had turned in, Leni lingered in her chair with her work; Calhern stood looking into the fire, one arm on the mantel. "Is the town really so dead?" he asked. "Seems to me there's plenty to do if you look around a little."

"Where do you look?" Leni was wide-eyed. "Or is that a question one ought not to ask?"

"No harm in asking. Well, just down your street there's a first-class museum. The symphony's starting up again in the fall. A beautiful park. Plenty of cafés. The hotel I stayed in has a place to dance that doesn't look too bad."

"Oh, I know the Kasteel. But I haven't been there in ages. Not since—" She broke off and picked at her embroidery.

"Did Wally Mills take you there?"

"No, never. The last time I went was four years ago. My cousin took me. It was my seventeenth birthday. Marshal Rommel was there, and the Gauleiter. They sat at our table for a minute and bought champagne for us."

Calhern stared. But as it came through Leni's prattle, the scene was touched with nostalgia, a vignette of brighter days.

"I'd always figured that Dutch people spent their time blowing up dikes or brooding by the hearth. You know the kind of stuff you imagine if you're not on the spot." He smiled. "Somebody told me once that Paris nightlife was hottest during the Reign of Terror."

"Oh, at first we had no reign of terror. Later it was different, when people hadn't enough to eat, and there was all the business with the Jews. But at the beginning, the Germans behaved well. They tried to make up for the bombing, which wasn't too bad actually. It was the fire more than the Germans that destroyed the city."

Calhern doubted these distinctions were her own; she seemed as impervious to irony as a doll. "You must have seen a lot of them."

"Of the Germans? Oh yes. But surely Papa has told you."

"Told me what?"

"He had a brother in the army, and several nephews."

"Were they captured by the Germans?"

"No, no, they were in the Wehrmacht. One branch of Papa's family comes from Dusseldorf. My German cousin was stationed here. Hugo was in the Engineers, so they put him in charge of the beaches and forts at Scheveningen. He wasn't old but he was very clever. It was Hugo who took me dancing at the Kasteel." She pushed back the curtain of her hair; her blue eyes clouded. "Poor Hugo—he had your room, you know."

Calhern gazed into the fire. "And what happened to him?"

"Oh, Hugo is dead."

Calhern pulled himself up short. He didn't want to say he was sorry. And the vision of Leni in the arms of the young lion, stopping in the park while his mouth covered hers, climbing perhaps into the bed he now occupied—that he couldn't stomach. The waste of body and spirit he had lived through in North Africa and Italy still gnawed at him; he couldn't fit any German officer into the context of his own youth. Then he remembered that Leni was just seventeen when Marshal Rommel bought her champagne. It would have been gross— profane, really—to sour her memories with the catechism of the liberators.

"Why not give the Kasteel a whirl ourselves? I mean why not go dancing there some night?"

"Oh, I should love it."

"How about next Monday?"

"Wonderful! I shall ask Mama."

"You think she might object?"

"I don't think so. It's just the way we do things. My parents will want me back by eleven." She reddened. "You'll think us dreadfully old-fashioned."

As she got up, the log in the fire collapsed with a shower of sparks. "No, not all," Calhern said. "It's just that in the last few years I've forgotten a lot of things."

On Monday Calhern glanced up from his files to see Engineer Rohrabach in the waiting room. Huge and tweedy, he towered over the other rain-soaked applicants like the ghost of middle-class Rotterdam. When Calhern opened the glass doors, his landlord came marching down the rows of desks like a captain among galley slaves. He clicked his heels and held out a paw.

"I have come to find out about going to your country."

Calhern slid the doors shut and placed a chair. "What a surprise!" he said. "Business? Pleasure? A long stay?"

"That depends on many things." Rohrabach wiped the raindrops from his forehead. "You may recall that we spoke the other night of the Schermerhorns in New York."

"Yes."

"Schermerhorn may need more engineers in his refineries."

"Ah, then Leni and your wife would go with you?"

"Later perhaps. I might make a short visit to look around first. I wanted to talk with you before we decide."

"The trouble is that the quota for immigrants is used up. You'd have a year's wait. But if you go as a visitor, you can't stay. You have to leave the States and start waiting all over again."

Rohrabach raised an eyebrow, as though he had caught a junior engineer palming off a faulty design. "I'm told that some visitors manage to stay all the same."

"It's been done, but it's not legal. It's unfair to the others who have to wait. No harm in your registering, though; we can screen you right away while you make up your mind." He fished out a form and pushed it across the desk. "You should get a letter from Mr. Schermerhorn about the job. You'll need a birth certificate, military records, and so on. And from The Hague a certificate of political reliability."

Rohrabach sighed. "The war has reduced everything to absurdity. How, may I ask, do the Americans measure reliability?"

Calhern smiled at this echo of his chief. "Maybe it's absurd, but right now that's how we have to operate. No Nazis, hard or soft; no communists, fascists, anarchists—you name it."

"Most commendable!" The blunt, manicured fingers folded the form over twice. "I can see no difficulty. But I mustn't keep a busy man from such important work."

In the waiting room, Rohrabach's gaze came to rest on the old mantelpiece, above which the tiles were inscribed in Dutch: "East, West, Home is Best."

"It's a strange slogan for immigrants, isn't it?" Calhern said.

The Engineer gave a laugh that was more like a bark. "Very Dutch," he said, "but the owner of this house would find it even more ironic than you do."

Calhern knew that the owner was lodged behind barbed wire at the edge of the city. "Yes, I've heard about Mynheer Willems."

"Sad, all that: misunderstandings, injustice. But no one in Holland has quite recovered his sanity." He looked around. "We've spent many evenings in this room. Quite a place in the old days."

"I hope the new tenants are not too much of a comedown." Calhern instantly regretted his words.

Rohrabach gave him a mournful, marble stare. "The Americans would never be unwelcome, my dear fellow."

Calhern felt a stirring of mistrust. They stood looking through the long windows at the garden, all matted in the rain, and the gray river beyond.

"One other thing." Rohrabach held out his hand. "I'd rather you said nothing to my wife for the moment. Or to Leni."

"I never talk shop outside the office."

In the dining room of the Hotel Kasteel, Calhern and Leni elbowed their way through the crowd that revolved in a viscous mass around the narrow dance floor. Once they were settled at their table, they

had to shout at one another above the loud talk and the clash of cut-
lery and the thumping tangos and jazz. Calhern wondered whether
Mevrouw Rohrabach was aware of the social dosage to which he was
exposing her daughter. Magnates of the black market and their
women, piano-legged and horn-rimmed even in prosperity; sober-
suited burghers and their grayish wives, with their noses tilted scorn-
fully in the smoky air; officers, soldiers, sailors, black, white, and
yellow; whores with irridescent eyelids under the brims of their man-
nish fedoras—all barriers were down.

Calhern ordered a sole and then a huge pancake covered with
apples. Nix on the champagne: he couldn't hope to compete with
Marshal Rommel, and Dutch gin and beer would fuel them better
for the mob on the dance floor.

Leni's technique startled him: cheek glued to cheek, heavy work
with belly and knees in the tango dips. If her German cousin had
taught her to dance like that, he had apparently left her with no idea
of the effect on the male animal. But there was nothing insidious
about Leni. Mills had been right: she had budded but not ripened;
there was room for development. The little round breasts that lifted
her silk blouse were like early fruit, and when she shook out her
yellow hair, she seemed unconscious of exploiting an asset. The
women he had known in Brussels and Paris carried themselves with
a discreet emphasis that let you know you could score without protestations. Leni remained a schoolgirl, and while Calhern felt no
desire for reckless commitments, he was happy to recover in her
something of his own past.

"What was it that happened to your cousin Hugo?" he asked as
the band began beating out a slow waltz.

She drew back in his arms, but without missing a step. "He was
killed at Scheveningen: a mine that went off by mistake. It was too
horrible."

"I don't know what made me ask."

But Leni's transitions covered any gaffe. "Mama and Papa were
heartbroken—Mama especially. She rather fancied Hugo—I mean
for me, of course. And the next man was not nearly so nice."

"The next man?"

"The one they quartered on us. He was an engineer too. We always seemed to draw them—I suppose on account of Papa. They never stopped talking to each other about some big project near The Hague. It was a terrible bore."

"But with your cousin it was different."

"Yes." She hesitated for an instant. "I know what you're thinking, but it wasn't that, Mr. Calhern. How can I explain without sounding silly."

"You might start by calling me Tom."

"Okay then: Tom." Her cheek brushed his and she gave a little laugh. "Hugo came from a better family than the other one. He was much younger and less touchy—about politics, I mean. He had to do what he was told naturally, but he wasn't a real Nazi. He knew us better: he was more like a guest."

Calhern had heard a dozen times how the Dutch hosts gnawed on beetroots or passed out in the street. "Your guests didn't appreciate your hospitality much," he said.

When they were back at their table, Leni, flushing a bit, said, "You really ought not to take it seriously, Tom, that we had Germans in our home. Where in Holland weren't there Germans?"

And now where weren't their Americans or British? No use kidding himself: he wasn't any more of a guest than the Germans had been—or the French or the Spanish. But for Leni the whole business was personal: she had only shades of sympathy to mark her frontiers, and it wasn't decent to infer anything else from the scrawled slate she had held up for him to see.

"I don't take it seriously, Leni." He glanced at his watch. "And speaking of home, it's almost midnight."

Leni paled. "Heavens! Mama will be in a state."

On the following evening he came in to find Mevrouw Rohrabach lying in wait in the salon. She beckoned him in with an air of conspiracy and cornered him on the leather sofa. When she had poured him coffee, she sat twisting her ringed fingers.

"Leni," she said finally, "is a bit anxious about last night."

"Oh?" He grasped the slippery arm of the sofa. "I hope nothing was wrong. I'm sorry we were late. It was my fault entirely."

"It's nothing awful. We know you are a serious young man, Mr. Calhern. And Leni had a marvelous time: quite like the old days. But she doesn't know how to repay your kindness."

Calhern smiled: for Leni the old days didn't stretch back very far. "There's nothing to repay. I had a good time too."

"I'm so happy to hear it." Mevrouw Rohrabach raised her eyes to his: he caught just a fleeting glint of malice. "Leni has asked me to help her—she's a bit shy, you know—and quite by chance I find that I can. I have an invitation for you."

"From Leni? I didn't know she was so shy."

"Well, it's not exactly from Leni. It's for both of you, from an aunt of my husband in Warmond. The Baroness"—she faintly underlined the word—"is giving a small dance for some officers who have just returned from Indonesia. Friday next. I do hope you are free."

Calhern had a feeling he had been ambushed; the social calendars of vice-consuls were not heavily charged. And he suspected that if he refused, it wouldn't help Leni much. "I'm free," he said, and then with tinsel enthusiasm, "I'd be delighted; it sounds great."

"Oh, Warmond is not Paris," Mrs. Rohrabach trilled, "but the house is charming. You will see a little of the old Holland. Of course it is a bit far, and we have no car."

"I'm sure my boss will let me take a jeep."

"What fun! *Voilà qui est reglé.*" She got up briskly, as though he might elude her at the eleventh hour. "We do like Leni to have a good time. We don't want all her memories of Holland to be sad."

"Memories?" Calhern got up. "Mynheer Rohrabach has told you about his plans then."

Her veined eyelids dropped. "My dear boy, what's a wife for if not to discuss plans? And you were so kind with the visa."

The past tense struck him as airy. "I hope," he said with emphasis, "that everything will be all right."

She gave a moue which in younger days had no doubt proven irresistible. "I had understood from Teo that it was all settled."

"Not until it's signed and sealed." Why did the Rohrbachs always make him sound pompous? "I'm sorry, but that's how it goes with visas."

Patting her curls, Mevrouw Rohrabach rallied her optimism. "I'm sure you will find a way to help us. And of course it's important for Leni—for her future, I mean."

Calhern stared through the window at the barges ploughing up and down the Great Canal. "I'll do what I can."

"Oh, do!" cried Mevrouw Rohrabach. "We are counting on you."

The Rohrabach papers arrived at Calhern's desk a few days later. The Schermerhorns had provided a cagily worded offer of support. The Dutch bureaucracy had authenticated the past: birth, baptism, residence, innocence of crime. And the document at the bottom of the pile declared, over a florid scrawl and the seal of the security police, that about the politics of Teodor Rohrabach and his wife Gertrude, residing at Keizerstraat 38, nothing unfavorable appeared in the files.

Calhern turned this paper over several times, holding it to the light as if to make out some cryptogram in the brief, bland text.

He started to call the Consul General, and then, with his finger still in the dial, he saw that he would have to divulge the source of his doubts. Did Leni's involvement really matter? He found, to his dismay, that it mattered a lot. He put the phone back on its cradle and tossed the file into the box marked "Pending."

In return for cigarettes, the Consul General's chauffeur had tuned up the second-best jeep for the trip to Warmond. The roar of brick pavement under the tires discouraged conversation, and Leni, after a few tentative chirpings, tucked her chin into her coat collar and surrendered to the buffeting wind. So they rolled along for over an hour until the old village appeared, sharp on the darkening horizon.

The house was a baronial relic: solid stories and jelly-roll gables planted athwart a sandy avenue, lined with the wispy poplars that fill the landscapes of Hobbema. The interior was no disappointment: great rooms opening into one another, wainscotted in oak, which two centuries had rubbed to buttery smoothness. There were acres of parquet, glistening in the candlelight, and tapestried chairs, and towering cupboards surmounted by blue jars.

The Baroness was of a piece with the house: a fragile, silvery old woman in black, who really should have been wearing a ruff. She pecked Leni on either cheek and pumped Calhern's hand twice, welcoming him tersely in a deep, husky voice. He could have embraced her for abstaining from the usual tribute to the liberators. Here at last was the Europe he had hoped to find when he left the hotel, with a Dutch woman capable of judging her country's latest deliverance on her own terms.

The rooms were thronged with bud-lipped girls, in pale, fluffy dresses, and horsy young Dutchmen, many still in khaki or blue. Some of the faces were scrubbed and ruddy; others were still pallid from the concentration camps of Java. Calhern felt incongruous—the city slicker in the manor. But the great-aunt and Leni's friends soon put him at his ease. Three fat musicians—accordion, piano, violin—pulled, thumped, and scraped: mostly polkas and waltzes, which he danced with more gusto than skill. Leni was much in demand, but he didn't lack for other partners. An ancient butler, with his white tie askew, shuffled about with punch and cakes, and at midnight the Queen was toasted with sour champagne.

After that Leni hunted him out. Her upper lip was beaded with sweat, and she gave off a faint musk of exertion. She led him onto the balcony overlooking the garden, where the buttresses of the brick wall swam in the dimness like the beams of a galleon. Calhern saw that she was uneasy: Cinderella awaiting the fateful strokes.

"We've a long trip to make, Tom."

"Whenever you say." He mopped his brow. "How about one more polka for the road? I'm just beginning to catch on. I'd like the last dance to be with you. Your mother won't worry, will she? After all, your aunt can vouch for you."

"I hope you don't always take Mama literally."

"Why not? She told me I'd enjoy it here, and she was right."

"No, no, I mean about me—all that business about me being too shy to invite you. When she told me that," Leni added in a burst of unfilial frankness, "I said she really mustn't exaggerate so."

"Why didn't you just ask me yourself?"

"I wasn't sure I really ought to. But Mama is more clever."

"You mean she thought I might escape? But why should I want to escape from you, Leni?"

She put her arm through his. "Oh, if it were only me— "

"What in God's name are you driving at?"

"It's all of us. We count so heavily on you."

Shades of her mother! But what a difference! "If you're talking about going to the States—about the visa—what can I tell you? You'll just have to be patient."

"I'm not impatient. It's Papa who is in a hurry. He means to talk to you about it again. And very soon."

Calhern wished he could put his hands over his ears. "Well, until he does talk, why don't you and I just forget about it? We've got better things to talk about."

"No, no, I must tell you. You must know everything if you're going to help us. It wouldn't be right to hide anything." She took a deep breath. "Papa has many rivals, as you can guess. Some of them are rather envious of his career—of his success, I mean."

"What can they do about it?"

"They have powerful friends in The Hague, and they've begun to spread stories about his work during the war. It's what I told you before: forts and missile places and so on. The *procureur* may even open an investigation."

Calhern put his hand over hers. "Excuse me, Leni, but you're not helping your father by telling me these things. I shouldn't say this, but just between us, nothing shows in any of his papers. Anyway, I wouldn't think dashing off to the States would do him much good either."

"Perhaps if he is no longer here, people will find someone else to be beastly to—at least that's what Papa thinks."

Calhern remembered the Consul General's prognosis. "I don't suppose it's the end of the world anyway. But doesn't he want to hang around long enough to clear himself?"

Leni withdrew her hand from his. He saw that he had been crude, but he counted on her straightness. "I'm not sure he could clear himself," she said. "When it comes to the Occupation, everyone is a little crazy: we're worse about our own people than we are about the

Germans. Look what happened to the poor man who owned your consulate." For a minute her upturned face was that of a stranger; her resignation reached depths he hadn't imagined in her range, and he was alarmed for her. "Suppose Papa does clear himself. Who do you think will ever remember only that?"

"Maybe it's not all that terrible. But let your father and me handle the American end. No need to drag you into it."

"I'm dragged in already. I'm up to my neck. Ever since you came, Papa and Mama have been—well, surely you understand why we're both here tonight."

"Didn't you want me to come here, Leni?"

"Dear Tom, don't pretend to be stupid. Of course I wanted you to come. But see what I've got you into: it complicates everything."

"Not unless you want it to. Don't you know that I trust you completely?"

"Oh trust! That's very nice, but it's not much good to me."

He stood breathing the frugal perfume that floated up from the garden. "Please try to forgive me, Leni. I'm sorry, I had no idea— "

"I was afraid that's what you would say." When she turned toward the window, he saw that her cheeks were wet.

In the drawing room the Baroness was taking a rest in a high-backed chair, enthroned in a circle of youth, their faces shining in the light of the candles, which had begun to gutter in their sconces. She rose with the men, and there was a round of bows and handshakes and clicked heels as the outlanders took their leave. She went with them to the portico and stood in the triangle of light from the open door while Calhern stammered his thanks in Dutch, to which the old woman replied in kind, with just a nod of her silvery head, as if he had spoken her language all his life. When the great door shut behind them, the night insects in the grass took up again their soft shrilling.

In the hall of the pension the nightlight glimmered in its red glass. Leni glanced at the clock, suspended in the arms of a Dresden shepherdess. *"Hemel!"* she whispered, "it's after two."

She stood there, motionless. Almost without thinking, Calhern, as if to efface the smear of shame that their talk had left, leaned down and, taking her chin between his fingers, kissed her gently on the mouth. Her lips lingered on his, and in a rush of warmth, he lifted his arms to embrace her. Just then he heard, from the darkness at the far end of the hall, the whine of an unoiled hinge and a faint click.

He turned sharply: there was no one and no light under the doors. All in an instant he had dropped his arms; they were numb, as though circulation had stopped. He whispered a good night and tiptoed away. Groping for the handle of his door, he looked back. Leni stood in the flickering red of the nightlight. Her shadow leaped enormous on the wall, but she had not moved at all.

Brushing past the clerks, the Engineer strode through the waiting room and flung open the sliding doors. Calhern's heart skipped a beat, but Rohrabach's good morning was cheerful. He sat down without ceremony.

"I have come to find out whether my papers are in order."

"I've looked at them all." He swallowed. "I'm sending them up to the Consul General today."

"Part of your routine, I suppose."

"Not always. But I'm new at the game, and the chief has dealt with documents and regulations all his life."

"And with the bureaucrats who provide them, no doubt."

Calhern looked up. "Exactly," he said.

The Engineer's large, clean hands were folded serenely in his lap. His linen coat and yellow vest, old-fashioned but impeccably cut, were freshly laundered. His face shone with health. For a minute Calhern thought that the dark shadows Leni had traced must be a dream.

"Your chief will know then, Mr. Calhern, what value to attach to all that paperwork. But you look doubtful. Is something missing?"

"The political certificate seems sketchy; it doesn't really say anything. Maybe you can fill it out a little—especially if you expect to move permanently to the States."

"Aha! You see me as a fellow citizen. I'm highly flattered. For the time being, though, I think of myself more as a tourist." He leaned forward. "But what more can I tell you?"

"Can you tell me anything about the war years?"

"You refer, no doubt, to the Occupation. Well, nothing much happened to me: I wasn't young enough."

Calhern saw pitfalls in the underbrush of Rohrabach's reticence and of his own. He sought a path around them, sought so intensely that he nearly lost sight of the imposing figure across the desk.

"You kept on with your work? Was it a success?"

"It didn't go badly. It wasn't always easy, I can tell you."

"Did you have help?"

"I'm not in the habit of asking for help."

"But you had connections in Germany—relatives in the Wehrmacht. Isn't that right?"

Rohrabach's eyelids sharpened. "You've been pumping my daughter."

"Oh pumping! I've talked with Leni, sure. Why not? She's told me nothing there's any point in trying to hide."

"To hide from *you*—well, perhaps not." The Engineer gave a mirthless guffaw. He threw himself back in his chair, spreading a hand on his knee as if lecturing a grandchild. "Put yourself in my place, Mr. Calhern; try to see things like a Netherlander. We had to live; we couldn't all survive on tulip bulbs. And we had families. At times we made concessions: we did things we didn't much like. That does not mean we were Nazis."

"I didn't say you were a Nazi, Mynheer Rohrabach."

"You've gone to a great deal of trouble to avoid the word."

"Okay, let's use it. Not all Hollanders did what the Nazis wanted."

"My dear fellow, you must not take offense if I say that you are not very experienced. Do you really believe that all my compatriots fought as they now claim to have fought? Those who did resist had perhaps less to lose than the others."

Calhern stared at the gold watch chain that girdled the evidence of the Engineer's survival. "Lots of them are dead."

Rohrabach's cheeks darkened. "And so no politicians are interested in blackening their names."

"And none of them wants to go to the United States."

The Engineer rose, planting his knuckles on the edge of the desk. "I should like to see the Consul General."

"I'll ask for an appointment," Calhern said. "At your risk, of course."

"My risk?" Rohrabach's pupils dwindled to dark points. "If your chief has had so much experience, he is probably familiar with the ways of vice-consuls too, eh?"

"Are you going to get Leni mixed up in all this mess?"

"Leni is a very innocent girl. My wife has had a long talk with her." Rohrabach folded his arms. "Perhaps you don't realize how simple Hollanders interpret your behavior."

"I'm the simple one; I can see that. Maybe it's your wife who should talk to the Consul General." Then Calhern saw the greater danger: his bitterness drained away. "Isn't it really Leni who could set the record straight?"

The Engineer sat down again, slumping forward on his chair. Some protective impulse, some tenderness welling up from depths that Calhern had never expected to fathom, washed at the layers of guile that the years had deposited at the corners of Rohrabach's eyes. The expression came and went in an instant, like the shadow of a cloud, but without it, he would never have known the Engineer at all. Now at last he understood how the Germans had melted down their foes into accomplices when they assembled their hostages at the sites marked throughout the city with little crosses and withered flowers.

"Look," Calhern said, "I don't expect Leni to do anything like that. I wouldn't want her to. And I'm sure you wouldn't either."

"I would rather not budge from Rotterdam."

"But why should I refuse the visa?" Calhern said softly, almost to himself. "The papers are all in order."

Rohrabach's chin jerked up: didn't he grasp yet that the cage stood open? "What about your chief?" he asked.

"He won't mind if I take a gamble on my own. It's about time."

"Mr. Calhern, are you in love with my daughter?"

"I might have been"—he brought it out slowly—"if I'd been given half a chance. But it was finished before it could really begin. You don't give me credit for much, do you? This business you and your wife cooked up—did you really think it would work?"

This time the Engineer's smile was not ironic. "The war has taught us new habits, you see, but maybe they are just new kinds of naiveté."

"You can pick up your passport tomorrow." They both stood up. "I may not see you again, Mr. Rohrabach. I wish you luck. Really."

Rohrabach gripped his hand. Then he turned away and crossed to the sliding doors, pushing them slowly apart, like Samson heaving against the pillars of the temple. He looked back once. "You are the lucky ones," he said. "You can still make such choices."

By the time Calhern had finished his report, twilight had come down. A breeze from the river stirred the papers on his desk. He stapled the Rohrabach dossier together with a thump and tossed it into his "Out" box. As he was locking his safe, the Consul General looked in.

"Working late again. Anything wrong?"

"Nothing. My landlord is going to the States. Family later."

"Problems?"

"Nothing serious. A little fuzzy for the war years, but I'm not hunting for trouble on this one."

The chief's glance stopped just short of a wink. "Good man," he said. "You'll be moving then. Let me know if you need help finding a place."

Calhern didn't answer for a moment. "Thanks," he said finally. "I'll be all right."

From outside the door of the Pension Rohrabach he heard women's voices rising and falling, first separately and then together. When he opened the door, there was a squeak of panic from down the hall, and he caught a glimpse of Mevrouw's curls whisking out of sight as she took refuge in her bedroom.

He bathed his face and packed his bags as meticulously as if he were journeying to the end of the world. Presently he heard the clicking of officious heels; the front door slammed and there was silence. But when he tiptoed into the hall, Leni stood there waiting. She wore the thin housedress he remembered from his first evening at the pension. She had drawn her hair back so tight that her eyes narrowed at their corners, but he couldn't see any trace of tears.

"I just wanted to thank you," she said, with a stiff little nod that reminded him of her aunt, "and to tell you—to tell you how happy you have made us."

"*You* don't look very happy."

"No more do you." Now the words came all in a rush. "Believe me, dear Tom, it wasn't my idea to threaten you. I am ashamed, ashamed!"

"I thought you knew me better, Leni."

"Don't go on. I know it's dreadful, what they've made you do. I have had a terrible quarrel with Mama about it. But what can I say?"

He reached out and touched her neck. "You don't understand: there's nothing dreadful. It wasn't because of any threat that I gave your father his visa. I have nothing against your father."

"But you do. You have everything." She drew away from him, clenching her hands together, shaking her head like an insistent child. "You learned it from me. And if you had waited, you would have learned it from others."

"I didn't want to wait."

"So then"—she marshaled all the logic of her simplicity—"so you have made an exception out of kindness."

"Oh, kindness! Dear Leni, you're the one who makes all the exceptions." She turned this over, and Calhern saw from her face that he had better extinguish the spark before either of them could breathe on it. "Everything is okay, okay. Stop worrying about it. Otherwise you'll get me worrying too." He took her hands in his. "And now I really must be going."

"You're leaving us?"

He couldn't help smiling. "Well, I don't think your father will put me in charge of the pension. And of course, you and your mother will be leaving too, one of these days."

"You won't stay to say goodbye?"

"I don't think I'd better. I'll send the driver for my bags as soon as I find something."

"I understand." Now at last her eyes filled. "I shan't see you again."

"Oh, I'll be around." He groped for a formula. "Who knows? Maybe I'll see you in the States."

She withdrew her hands from his, as though she didn't dare to press on a surface so fragile. If only she would yell at him, or throw something. Or hit him in the face. But of course she wouldn't, and her abstention was worse than any reproach.

"Many thanks, Leni," he said, "for everything—most of all for just being you."

She turned away without a sound.

Along the Great Canal, the arc lights bobbled on their wires, stabbing the black water with their reflections. Bars and dance halls hoisted their impudent emblems to the wind: from one of them a party of sailors erupted in disorder. They shouted and peered at Calhern and then up and down the street, like marine creatures stranded by the tides that were ebbing all around them. At the bend of the canal, the towers of the Hotel Kasteel came into view: their windows twinkled above the wreckage, as oblivious as the stars.

He would find no comfort there, no refuge from the desolation that worked within him, and around him. But really, he told himself, there was nowhere else for him to go.

Famous Trials

Old Dr. Chisholm, who had given the freshman hygiene lectures for two generations, was unaccustomed to epidemics. His Harvard practice consisted mostly of broken arms, colds, diarrhea, and, despite his vivid warnings, an occasional dose of clap. These could be treated at the Dispensary, and proper Bostonians went home when they took really sick. But I was an outlander: my parents in the Midwest were a day and a half away by train. When a wave of mononucleosis swept through the Yard dormitories, I couldn't just hop a plane and announce that I was "coming down" with something.

Dr. Chisholm thrust a thermometer under my tongue. While the mercury climbed, he palped my neck and my crotch abstractedly. "Still another one. No doubt about it."

"Another what, sir?"

"We don't *know* what." His tone was plaintive but not unkindly. "Oh, we've found a fancy name: mononucleosis. But what does that mean? In these glandular things, there's always an x-factor." He pulled his glasses down from his forehead and squinted at the thermometer. "Feeling rotten?"

"Yes, sir."

"Stillman Infirmary for you." My heart sickened. "You'll feel worse before you feel better." He scribbled illegibly on a form, his turkey jowls wobbling, and thrust it at me with a wink. "Next man!"

The Infirmary was a good mile from the Yard. It looked more like a dormitory than a hospital: red brick with the Tudor trimmings dear to academic architects, and long, vertically bisected window frames that gave the building a permanent frown, as if it were ashamed of its function. The halls smelled of phenol, and in the overheated room where I stowed my clothes in an olive-green locker, I began to wonder whether I would ever get back to the world of History I, and hour exams, and Glee Club, and peanut butter and bacon sandwiches. Naked and shaking with chills, I waited there until an orderly handed me a rectangular cake of cloth, which unfolded into cotton pyjamas and bathrobe, bleached almost to transparency.

Once I had pushed my way into this cocoon, the orderly took me to the top floor in a clanking elevator and turned me over to Miss Corrivau, the ward nurse. While I tried to clench my chattering teeth, she made the first entry on the chart at the foot of my bed. She watched me roll myself into a ball under the blanket and then warned me to steer clear of other patients. "They're full down in Contagious, so we take a few of you up here." Her smile was enigmatic, her accent faintly exotic. Mona Lisa, I thought: I was only nineteen.

Tucking her shining, reddish hair under her cap, Miss Corrivau made off down the ward, starched skirts swinging. When she passed the hall door, her slimness was silhouetted against the brighter light.

By the time supper trays had come around, I had entered the burning phase, where, except for brief swoops into subnormal shivers, I was to remain for many days. As I sat picking at boiled scrod and raspberry jello, waves of heat broke over me, mounting in swift succession to my forehead. I sought distraction in conversation with my neighbors: on the left, a pale wisp in steel-rimmed glasses, who confided in Georgian accents that he, too, was "glandulah"; on the right, a curly-haired husky of Sicilian aspect, with his leg in traction.

"Football?" I asked.

"No, squash. Doc Chisholm has knocked me out for the season." He had the shallow voice of an athlete and seemed mildly disgusted, but whether with me or the doctor I wasn't sure until he added, "I'm Balboni."

"Ah, Balboni!" I had failed to recognize the captain of varsity squash. I held out a fevered paw, as though to a film star and then, remembering Miss Corrivau's warning, withdrew it. "Tough luck," I said.

The Georgian wisp told me I was passing through the worst. "Sometimes you think the top of youah haid's comin' clean off." Later, he said, would come "the weak sweats." He was spending his convalescence growing a beard. When he turned his head to the light that was clamped to his bed, I made out a scruffy fringe of orange around and under his chin. "Omlee says it's comin' along fine. Be full grown when ah leave."

"Omlee?"

"Ah-mell-lee. Miss Corrivau. The doll who tucked you in. She's real nice. Not grouchy, like that ol' Mahoney."

The Sicilian remarked, in tones reserved for those who cheat at games, that the previous tenant of my bed had died.

"Died? Of mononucleosis?"

Heads turned toward us from the other beds. "It turned into pneumonia," the Georgian said. "They trahd that new sulfa stuff. Didn't touch this fellow at all."

And they told me how my predecessor, a law student named Pell, had been wheeled off to "the room" at the end of the hall, but not before the ward had heard the beginning of his panting agony and the trundling of the oxygen cart.

I pushed back my tray and closed my eyes. "No one dies at nineteen, *voyons,*" I told myself in the scoffing manner I had come to admire in my French instructor. But it was several minutes before I found the nerve to swing my legs out from under the coarse sheets and totter off, in the Infirmary's paper slippers, to the bathroom.

Amelie Corrivau scanned my chart doubtfully before she confirmed my "bathroom privileges." I think she gave them to me because Miss Mahoney, the night nurse, did not approve. Miss Mahoney, whose mouth often puckered all around as though drawn by a cord, was a devotee of the bedpan. But she was junior in service, though certainly not in years, to Miss Corrivau, whose Quebec origins and slightly highfalutin manner caused scowls and mutterings.

I was thankful for this demi-feud but alarmed by the cotton in my legs whenever I dragged myself down the hall to the bathroom. The slatted half-doors were like those of a saloon; the place smelled of green soap and, mysteriously, of heated cardboard. There was something nightmarish about the outsized brass faucets and nick-eled shower pipes and the cold, rattling toilet seat on which I perched, with my hands dangling between my knees, because I was too weak to piss standing.

Near the main staircase, a tall window looked down into Mount Auburn Street. Here I often stopped to cool my cheeks against the glass and listen to the ding-dinging of the trolley cars. Through the thinning autumn foliage, I saw the clapboard cube of Elmwood. Its windows flared in the sunset, and the spirit of James Russell Lowell seemed to come and go with the little cloud of my breath on the windowpane. I wondered whether I would ever join the awesome circle of the Cambridge literati.

Across the hall was an unnumbered door. Unlike those of the private rooms, it was kept closed and had no signal bulb over it.

During my worst days, if Miss Corrivau saw me in the hall, she helped me back to bed, slowing down to offer me her arm. Her coppery hair gave off a faint odor of violet toilet water, and her shoes squeaked slightly against the linoleum. Sometimes I'd lie in wait behind the saloon doors until I heard that sound in the hall; I got so that I could tell her squeak from those of the other nurses. Peering through the slats, I'd watch her white figure approaching and then come out, tottering a little more than I needed to. She never had much to say: a few comforting words about my temperature; the autumn weather; an offer of orange juice. Her accent was flat like mine but not midwestern; there were overtones of Quebec in her vowels ("Air you better?"), and when the *r* of "orange" lingered momentarily in her throat, I heard echoes of a faraway alien world. I told her I might major in French. But she refused to practice with me. "Your professors would not like it if I gave you the *accent du*

Québec," she said with a touch of acidity.

Once in a while, after she had taken my pulse, her fingers, long and cool, stayed on my wrist. Or she'd lay them on my hot forehead before she went off on her rounds. Her touch caused a turmoil in my blood. "Or-range, or-range," I said to myself when she had gone.

As my illness continued, Cambridge and the Yard seemed farther and farther away. I found it hard to concentrate on the textbooks that my roommates had left for me. I kept dozing off when I struggled with Hazen's *Modern Europe*; or I'd push away *La Petite Fadette* and join the Georgian at the back window. We could see the steel-smooth Charles beyond the trees and the racing shells skittering past the boat house. The oarsmen bent and straightened and bent in unison, oars flashing in the sun until they dipped and swept again and then disappeared around the curve. In my weakness, I found their rhythmic flailing as bizarre as the motions of marine protozoans glimpsed for an instant in the world of the microscope.

One Saturday there was a race. Spectators lined the banks, and the syncopated cries of the coxswains floated up to our window. I saw myself restored to health, in a crimson sweater, standing with Amelie at the water's edge. Now it was my turn to offer an arm, while we cheered and stuffed ourselves with popcorn.

When I lay awake in the dark, with my fingers engorged and twitching with fever, I watched reflections of headlights circling across the ceiling like the legs of a compass; I imagined Amelie pressed close to me in a speeding automobile late at night.

One afternoon in my second week, I sneaked down and knocked at the closed door at the end of the hall. There was no answer. I tried the handle. It was not locked. I shuffled in and shut the door, leaning against it until my eyes had adjusted to the dimness. The room was musty and silent, more like an attic than a hospital. The iron bed was higher and narrower than the ones in the ward; above it hung a set of intersecting glassine trapezoids, and at the head stood three tall cylinders crowned with cogged faucets. The bedside table was bare, but in one corner of the room I saw a leather suitcase, a Burberry raincoat, and a miniature radio.

On the windowsill I found several books: Underhill on torts; a Blackstone with marbly endpapers; Birkenhead's *Famous Trials* in red buckram, with blindfolded Justice on the cover, holding her scales and sword. I scanned the titles: "The Trial of Mary Queen of Scots," "The Veronica Murders," "Sir Roger Casement," "The Maybrick Poisoning." This beat Hazen or George Sand any day: I would take the book with me. Then I looked at the flyleaf: "Michael Pell, Cambridge, 1932," in thick, inky writing, elegant, with long, vertical letters. Below in block capitals: "Please return to Hastings Hall."

I stood for a minute by the window, watching the slow drip of rain from the metal sash, and the golden leaves bobbing like lanterns in the soft patter. The street was quiet except for the singing of tires now and then on the pavement. My fingers gripped the book. Suddenly my eyes filled with tears. I pressed my forehead to the glass, murmuring, "Death, death, death," over and over, until the syllable lost all meaning.

When Amelie stopped at my bed that evening it was already late. The Georgian and Balboni, who snored behind his screen, were asleep. My bedlight burned illicitly as I washed down my aspirin with orange juice and snuggled in with Birkenhead. "She went to the block as a queen," I read, "and her memory still lives as that of a beautiful, radiant, and unfortunate woman, sacrificed to the policy of an envious rival." Boy!

Amelie tweaked my toes and whispered that I looked better. I said maybe I was, and she cautioned me against overdoing. I smiled: the possibilities didn't seem boundless. She said she could use some rest too. Then as she adjusted my light, her eyes fell on the volume in my lap. I heard just a faint catch of her breath.

"Where did you find that?"

I paled and then blushed. "Down the hall."

She turned her watch bracelet; her forearms were covered with faint golden down. "You're not supposed to go into any of the rooms. Sometimes those patients are very ill."

"There was no one in there."

She didn't seem to hear me. "They're not to be disturbed."

"There was no one," I insisted.

Amelie thrust the thermometer under my tongue. When she felt for my pulse, her fingers trembled. "If there had been, I'd have to report it. But I ought to take the book back. It's not yours."

I mumbled angrily around my thermometer: "I wasn't going to steal it!"

While she read my temperature, she turned her head toward the light, which caught the gentle curve of her neck and glinted on her hair. "I know that," she said softly. "But you mustn't forget to put it back. It belonged to the law student."

"The one who died?"

"Yes. We moved his books in there with him, and then after he died, they cleaned out his locker and put everything together to be packed up." She reached up to adjust her cap, and I could see her breasts move. "I suppose you'll be leaving us soon." Her tone was hard, almost brusque.

"Not like him, I hope."

"That's not funny. You're lucky—you and all the others."

Behind the screen Balboni gave a little high-pitched groan in his sleep.

"Maybe we are. But it's crazy: the longer I stay here, the less I care about getting out."

"You shouldn't talk like that. It's not far to Christmas. You'll be going home, no?"

"I suppose so. Lots of work to catch up before that. And hour exams. Where will you be going, Miss Corrivau?"

"Oh, I'll stay here. I have no more family—not down here. Brothers and sisters in Rimouski"—again I heard the *r*—"but I don't get back to Canada very often."

I reflected for a minute. "The thing is, after you've been lying here awhile, you don't care much about what goes on without you. No classes; nothing to worry about for tomorrow. There's nothing left for you to decide."

Amelie pushed my hair off my forehead. "Hospitals are still hospitals. You're beginning to sweat. Good sign—but stay nice and warm. Don't do anything silly."

I could hear tears in her voice: I had stirred a memory. I wanted to take her hand and press it to my lips, but I didn't know how to go about it. Instead, I scowled at the engraving of the Queen of Scots receiving Lord Buckhurst: she smiled rather smugly, I thought, at the foreknowledge of her martyrdom.

"I won't go in there again."

Amelie patted my hand. "You can have ten minutes more, and then lights out."

That night I dreamed that all of us in the ward must make a choice: either we go deep down near the center of the earth and live there forever, or we stay above ground and live in the full light of day, with the constant presentiment of death.

Balboni and most of the others elect to stay on the surface. The Georgian and I, escorted by Miss Mahoney, frowning like Pluto, decide to go underground. We drop interminably in an open iron cage, as if we were miners, until at last we come out onto a paved expanse, vast but finite—a kind of pre-Columbian world, whose far edge is circumscribed by a gray cyclorama. The surface is dotted with houses and buildings, but all in raw cement blocks, as in an unfinished real estate development. Instead of sky, there is a crisscross of nickeled pipes above us; at our feet, the terrain bristles with pressure gauges and brass spigots. In the cyclorama I notice a fissure through which water darkly trickles. Is the weight of the world—all those layers of earth—too great? Is the immortality deal a sell?

It is twilight down here: there are no shadows. The Georgian and I wamble about (Miss Mahoney has vanished) until a white-robed figure flutters toward us from among the blank buildings. It is Mary Queen of Scots, but instead of her pearled wimple, she is wearing a nurse's cap, tightly crushed down on her hair. I run from her in panic and finally get back to the elevator shaft. The cage has gone up, but the dial over the entrance wavers: the elevator is in trouble. Just as I am struggling for breath to call up the shaft for rescue, the Queen rustles up behind me and puts a cold hand over my mouth.

My pyjamas were soaked with sweat, and when I groped wildly around me, even the sheets were wet. Balboni was growling at me to shut up, and the Georgian came around the screen and tugged gently at my arm. He pushed my buzzer. Lights winked on all down the ward. In a minute Amelie was helping me out of bed. She wrapped a blanket around me and pushed me into a wicker chair by the window. I sat there gasping and shuddering, while in two rapid sweeps, she stripped the sheets, damply billowing, from the bed, and then she and the Georgian turned the mattress.

She helped me change pyjamas. I asked her, in a whisper, if she thought I was going to die.

"Don't be silly! Your fever has broken." For the first time I noticed a slight cast in her wide-apart eyes. She pinched my arm. "You're getting better."

On Sunday I was subnormal, but weak and listless. Miss Mahoney, grumbling, brought me a hot-water bottle. Down below, a radio was blasting out religious music. My roommates came by: they promised to borrow a jalopy to haul me back to the Yard. I tried to discuss hour exams and Glee Club, but I could hardly wait for them to leave. In the evening I was ravenous: I asked for more boiled chicken and ate two scoops of ice cream. I roared through *Famous Trials*, saving "Landru" and "Crippen's Mistress" for next day.

After Dr. Chisholm had made his rounds, Amelie told me I was to stay on for a few days. "We don't want to run any risk. It's turned out so raw and weendy." Was she thinking of pneumonia?

"Maybe I'll get out of hour exams."

"You don't seem to mind very much."

"I don't mind at all."

She smiled. "Neither do I."

As my strength came back, I thought more and more about the unnumbered room. I had promised Amelie I wouldn't go in there, but the passage of my own crisis made that grim corner irresistible. I told myself it was time to return Michael Pell's property—even though it couldn't matter to him.

It was Friday evening. They had just taken Balboni out of traction, and Miss Mahoney was helping him take his first steps. "Celebration," he announced grandly. "Miss Mahoney says we can all have chocolate sundaes."

"I never said any such thing!" Miss Mahoney cried. "Now let's get on with it."

I thought Amelie must have left for the evening as usual. When I had taken a shower, I sneaked across the hall and pushed open the unmarked door.

Ameilie was sitting on the edge of the narrow bed, with her back to me. In the twilight her white uniform fused into the white of the bedspread. I started to leave, but without turning around, she called out softly, "Don't go, don't go." I stood there gripping the heavy book. "I knew you wouldn't keep your promise." Her voice was choked: for a minute I thought she was angry.

"You told me to bring back the book, didn't you?"

"You're talking like a child." Still she didn't move. "You can close the door."

I laid the book on the foot of the bed. When I had shut the door with a little click, I came back and stood behind her, my throat pulsing. Then I saw that her shoulders were shaking. I reached across the bed and touched her hair; she drew a shuddering breath, and her hand went up to mine, and I pulled off her cap and let the whole silky mass tumble over my fingers. I had never felt a woman's hair in my hands like that, so full and rich and yet coarse. The odor of violets floated into my nostrils.

"Did you love him a lot, Amelie?"

Her head dropped and she rocked on the edge of the bed, trying to stifle her weeping. "There was nothing I could do for him."

"Have you lost—haven't other patients died?"

"They weren't like Michael."

"What was he like then?" I asked, still sifting her hair. An absurd jealousy rose in me. "Was he good-looking?"

"Oh, what does it mean really—good-looking? He was very blond. Pale, but with a heavy beard. I used to help him shave; even when he was weakest, he wanted to be neat. Blue eyes—but dark, dark blue. A smile more around his eyes than his mouth. Even when he was most afraid, he still smiled like that."

"I don't see what more you could have done."

"I don't know—nothing maybe. I thought about calling in a priest: sometimes the sacrament brings people back; the oil, you know. But Michael had no religion really. He said he wasn't going to let himself die. And he kept asking for his books. So we brought them in here."

"And did he ever know?"

"Know what?"

"That you loved him."

She looked up into the glassine tent above us. "At the end I held him in my arms. I tried to help him with his breathing, propping him up and everything. He kept whispering to give him more air, even when I turned the oxygen up as far as it would go. I kissed him, and he said, 'Amelie, I think I'm better.' And then all in a second his eyes opened wide and he was gone. I felt as though I'd let him slip through my fingers."

She threw back her head and drew my hands down over her shoulders, pressing them against her breasts. When I kissed her neck, she lay back on the bed with a sob so loud that I thought someone in the hall would surely hear. I turned away.

"Don't go," she whispered. "Don't leave me. Please. I don't want to think about it any more." She pulled me down beside her and clasped her arms around my neck. One of my paper slippers fell softly to the floor. "Stay for just a minute. Don't say anything. Just let me hold you."

I put my arms around her, and we lay there like that in the gathering dark, almost without moving, for what must have been a quarter of an hour. The torrent into which she had swept me carried off my jealousy—everything but the knowledge of her grief. And as her sobs died away, so did the desire that had run curdling through me. I could hear the trolleys rumbling past and the whishing of rain against the window. When my lips touched the salt on her cheeks, I felt soothed and lifted, as though I had let her save me and so had brought her comfort.

Gently she loosed herself from my embrace. We both sat up on opposite sides of the bed. "A fine noodle I am." She started winding up her hair. "And as for you—"

"'As for you, you must be cra*zee*. What air you doing out of your bed?'"

She kissed me quickly on the mouth and stood up. When she had pinned on her cap, she leaned over and straightened the coverlet, tucking it in professionally with hospital corners. Her eye caught the book on the foot of the bed. She put it beside the others on the windowsill. "So you've finished. Was it good?"

"It was great. Poisonings, stabbings, burning up corpses—you have no idea, Amelie: I mean, all the terrible things people do to each other."

"When they stop loving, is that it?"

"Yes."

"But sometimes they don't stop, you know. That's no fun either."

I twisted the cord of my bathrobe. "There's that, too," I said sagely.

She laid her palm along my jaw for a second.

"Amelie, I—"

"Off you go now. I'll wait a little and fix my face: it certainly must need it." She opened the door and the light from the hall sliced into the room. "Coast is clear. Don't tell Mahoney I'm still here."

"Did you think I'd tell anyone?"

When I dug my clothes out of the locker on Monday, they were wrinkled and smelled of carbolic. My tweed jacket felt like the weight of the world on my shoulders.

In the hall I met Amelie. "You look fine today," she said. "If you'll just comb your hair, you'll be *du dernier chic.* Take care now. Don't study too hard."

"Don't worry. And Amelie, thanks a lot. For everything."

"It's not for you to do the thanking."

She rose on her toes with a rustle of starched skirts. I thought she was going to kiss me. Just then the Georgian popped out of the bathroom, fully dressed but with razor in hand. At the last minute he had lost his nerve and shaved off his orange beard. "Two new mono cases in the ward," he told us cheerily. "And plenty of football injuries. You-all got youah hands full, Omlee."

"Oh, don't I know!" When he had gone, she said, "We'll miss you. Don't forget to come back and see us."

We; us. I thought about that while I watched for my roommates at the Mount Auburn Street window. More leaves had fallen: I could see more of Elmwood, high and square and sad in the November sunlight. I tried to see myself as a bearded Lowell or Longfellow, breasting the waves of literature and life, sharing the knowledge of pain and dying and loving without hope. Already the ranks of the underworld were closing up behind me: Amelie's pronouns were the right ones. But though I wrapped her words in forgiveness, my mouth was dry with a toxin for which there was no antidote.

The Overlap

Our house stands at the midpoint of the long flight of steps that makes up the main street of Barjaux. From our terrace we look up to the Mairie, the church, with its hobnail steeple, and the fragments of fort which the villagers indulgently allow the Swiss occupants to call the château. Below us lie more houses, many of them crumbling shells with attics gaping at the sky, and then the path that winds down to the river. As in other mountain villages, the houses huddle together for defense against the blasts of the mistral, and the northern side of ours is tightly embraced by our neighbor's walls. The stones and mortar enclosing Mme. Cayrol are jointed imperceptibly into ours: no straight line divides us. Our southern frontier is more conventional: an open stretch of wire rather than a tangle of common masonry separates our garden from that of M. Gevaudan, our mayor.

Coming up the hill from the river in the late afternoon, Helen and I often pause (as our sixties rush past us, we pause more often on those interminable steps) until the western windows of our house catch fire above us in the sunset. The lower windows blaze up first, one after another, as if they were joined by fuses, like the chandeliers in a stage-set for Molière. The tiny dormer, which Cuquemelle, the albino carpenter, and Barnouin, the amorous mason, have installed in our attic, holds the light a few seconds longer than the others. As we resume our climb (Helen has kept thinner and more nimble than I), the watchdogs bay in relays, and the voices of late bathers float up to us, reverberating like bells from the surface of the river. The Mayor's dog Coca leaves her lair, which is half of a wine cask split down the middle, to sniff out the prospects for largesse from the wasteful Americans. Coca's chassis is dachshund, but other strains have given her long legs so that she seems to move on stilts. Sometimes Mayor Gevaudan himself, black curls flying, rushes past, clutching bundles of Communist leaflets in his arms. He singsongs, *"Bonsoir, 'sieur et 'dame,"* and runs to silence the scream of his telephone, which is Barjaux's chief link with the world of the valley. Now and then we hear murmuring from the Douarnez kitchen: Eulalie is pestling herbs for one of her potions. Her husband Amédée, red-eyed and tiny, buried in the folds of a cast-off jacket of mine, bumps his wheelbarrow, filled with weeds from our garden, down the steps, turning as he passes to whip off his cap. And as the twilight deepens, the peasants struggle up from the vineyards, and the shepherds from the moors with their goats, bells clanking, udders swinging.

Helen's hand brushes mine. Here in the hills, it is the hour of family reunion, of momentary idleness and unspoken affection. As we listen to voices from gardens and kitchens, we think of our daughter Eleanor, caught in the briers of New York. We hope for good news: about her health, her courses, her doctorate. Most of all we long for her to love and be loved, but we don't say much: only "Don't you wish she were here?"

In the beginning Helen had doubts about buying the house. She recognized that Barjaux, discovered by chance during a summer excursion, had become—especially for me—an incurable attachment. "But let's think it over." I knew what was passing before her inner eye: the long migration every June; the two of us climbing the eighty-seven steps, she darting ahead with groceries, while I came puffing after with bottles and books; the longer and longer intervals between walks on the moors; the fewer and fewer dips of gammer and gaffer in the river. A retired diplomat in Paris was one thing; a white-haired villager and wife holed up in the Cévennes, with an only daughter in New York, would be another. Eleanor would have to

scrimp even more on the crumbs we could provide, while the con-
clusion of her thesis on Lamartine remained, like Zeno's tortoise, in
that unbridgeable half-distance ahead. And Helen challenged me
with the sequel: how could we imagine that our city mouse or her
boyfriend Fred, who lived in the random universe of Jack Kerouac,
would ever maintain a pied à terre inherited on the other side of the
ocean?

"Anyway," she said, "boyfriends don't stay boyfriends forever.
They're apt to fade away, unless"—her gray eyes brightened—"unless they can be turned into husbands."

"Let's face it," I said. "Fred is not a permanent factor. He's a
wanderer: all those exits and alarms and excursions."

"Better Fred than the other lame ducks she's mothered. Or the
political firebrands. And he hasn't done badly with his sculptures."

"Sculptures! Wire and string. They may go over big in the
Broome Street lofts, but uptown—"

Helen bristled. "Who says they won't catch on uptown?"

"Don't get me wrong. I like Fred." (And it's true: I do—scruffy
beard, granny glasses, adenoidish mouth and all.) "It's just that I
don't see him as husband and father."

"How about just a father?"

"Good God!"

"Yes, good God. You see how old-fogey we are?"

"Either way we'd be on call, I guess."

"That's right. And if we have to help out two people instead of
one, how do we swing the upkeep at Barjaux?"

But when the agent wrote us that she had another offer, Helen's
misgivings shriveled in the blaze of my panic. We sent the down pay-
ment by return mail. And as we planned the restoration of the attic,
wooing the elusive Cuquemelle and Barnouin with flattery and
Pastis, I had secret visions of Eleanor installed under the new tiles.
And alone. She could stow her nine-by-five cards in the workroom
cupboard; she could rattle pots and pans with Helen (nothing can
stale the variety of their cooking) and water the geraniums and
gather the apricots. Her biting humor would surely spice up the
bland diet of retirement. I could see her honey-colored hair swinging

as she mounted the village steps in a loose-flowing summer dress. I could hear her high, clear voice pushing out French phrases for *Monsieur le Maire,* or for Mme. Cayrol and her grandson Raymond.

These *tableaux vivants* I did not share. Helen preferred to see Eleanor and Fred (or anyone) pinned to the mat of marriage; she dreamed of clusters of grandchildren to spoil.

Each of the three whitewashed rooms on our ground floor is supported by a separate cellar, hewn out of the hillside and vaulted in stone. Mme. Cayrol tells us that during the War of the Camisards, one of our predecessors kept Catholics hidden down there; for her, this man figures not as a *collabo* but as a hero. Marguerite Cayrol is one of the last Catholics in a village that was Protestant even under Richelieu.

"Today the château," she tells me, "is in the hands of heretics. And our mayor is a Communist."

"He's not what I'd call orthodox either."

"No, thank heaven he's not. *Un brave type,* M. Gevaudan: always out to help the village. But we keep you heretics buried at the other end of Barjaux, and we have the only cypresses in town." The sly, gap-toothed smile that our neighbor gives me is not that of a fanatic. "You must forgive our games. This is not Belfast, after all."

Except when grandsons come to visit, Mme. Cayrol is alone in the big house. M. Cayrol's name is inscribed on the plaque commemorating members of the Resistance who died at the stone bridge that crosses the River Cèze. Cayrol *fils* left the village before the war, when the silkworms disappeared and Parisians devoured the wine cooperatives. He runs a clothing store in Nîmes, but with little help from his boys.

Raymond, fresh-faced and husky as a soccer star, usually comes to his grandmother's from the university in Paris at midsummer. Except at mealtimes, Mme. Cayrol doesn't see much of him. He is on the river in his faltboat; by August his face and torso have turned caramel, and his ginger mustache, more luxuriant every year, is burned white. We often hear the whine of his motorbike as he rounds the hairpins of the road from the valley and erupts into the miniature square near the church, with a blue-jeaned girl on the pillion, clutching his flat midriff. Raymond has fascist leanings: he wears a *Jeune Nation* T-shirt. But in Barjaux, where politics is a sport, his affiliations are just a joke. So is his competition with the Mayor for the schoolmistress from Saint-Genest. Like Shakespeare's Dark Lady, Mlle. Claire is sallow, with wiry hair, but her big breasts make heads turn when she comes up the village steps.

Marguerite Cayrol reserves for Raymond the same masked tenderness that she gives to her flowers. She worries about his morals and disapproves of the schoolmistress. "Ah, Mademoiselle Claire," she says, weighting each syllable with irony, "What is a *demoiselle* doing on motorcycles? Or at meetings with men in that Mickey Bar? The Mayor's politics are his business. But the schoolmistress—what an example!"

Of the other grandson Mme. Cayrol rarely speaks. The Mayor tells us that Étienne suffers from *dépression nerveuse*: he has to spend more and more time at the asylum in Uzès. Sometimes his father brings him to the village: these are not happy days for his grandmother, who lives in dread of his wandering down to the river or waylaying girls on the paths across the moor. Now and then we hear raggedy shouting from the kitchen on the other side of our wall. Or we glimpse Étienne through our neighbor's gate: he stands motionless under the umbrella of a fig tree, his black eyes flickering over the passers-by. The villagers take him fishing; the Mayor invites him to the *pétanque* matches in the square; but the stigma of the loser is never erased from his long-chinned face.

This summer—our fifth in Barjaux—we wrestle, like Mme. Cayrol, with the complications of family reunion. One morning Helen overtakes her as she hobbles up to wait for the yellow truck of the postman. After the ritual exchange of "*ça va's*," my wife asks why Raymond has not arrived.

"Raymond, madame, is on maneuvers." Her jaw waggles. "In this republic of ours, everyone must do his service. Don't ask me for what."

"Perhaps he will come on leave?"

"Yes, in August. He may be allowed to stay on for the wine harvest. And for the hunting, of course, with M. Gevaudan. Grapes must wait for rabbits and partridges."

"And for the girls, I suppose."

"At Raymond's age it is hard to say which is of greater interest. And what about your family, madame?"

"Our daughter will come in August too. We've just had a letter."

Mme. Cayrol's face lights. "Ah, madame, what a pleasure for you both. As it will be for all of us, I am sure. Her first visit?" As if she didn't know! "But not her last, I hope."

"Let us hope."

Mme. Cayrol's bedroom is on the same level as ours: we hear her stirring on the other side of the wall. She moves slowly, slowly; often she groans or talks to herself. As she has no electric lights, she goes to bed early, and when the summer evening fades, we have to tiptoe in our bedroom.

All our windows open inward. Their little panes are framed in brown oak. The shutters have been stained to match, and no pair is like any other, so that to keep them from banging against the stones during the mistral, we have jury-rigged all manner of spikes and wedges on the walls. Viewed from outside, our windows make us feel proprietary; from inside, I tell Helen, they are magic casements: if they don't open on the foam of perilous seas, at least they admit us into a Van Eyck canvas: the blue-green of the Cèze as it winds through overarching gorges and forest at the bottom of the mountain.

Helen is less given to flights of fancy. She complains that our Renaissance perspective is bisected by the Mayor's television aerial, soaring shakily above his privy. Our British friends the Parkinsons, who live on the next mountain, advise us to take potshots at this landmark while M. Gevaudan is away at Party meetings. We snicker politely, but as outlanders we have no rights in the matter.

Like many communists of the Midi, M. Gevaudan is hospitable to all his subjects, including the two *Amerloques* (the local cell has not inoculated him), but he has little confidence in our durability. And he tunes in quickly to any condescension from city folk, whether or not they are Comrades. What would really make him happiest would be to turn the clock back half a century, to a point beyond his own memory. The villagers would return from the factories at Lyon and the atomic center at Pierrelatte; the summer folk—Swiss, Dutch, Parisian, American—would shutter their houses for good; the campers who litter the meadows with beer cans and scum the river with detergents would fold their tents forever. Prices of goat cheese and grapes would rise; M. Cayrol's sawmill would turn again. Coca would be taken out hunting every day, with a bit of poaching before the wine harvest. And he and his brother would have ten children each.

Before Eleanor arrives, Helen and I make bets on her preferences. Helen predicts that she will go for M. Gevaudan, the romantic rebel, with his glossy beard and his long, harried stride that takes the village steps two at a time. I put my money on Raymond's ginger mustache and unthinking laughter. As it turns out, both of us are wrong.

Here in Barjaux the telephone never rings, except for the poor mayor; his kitchen has become a public telephone booth and a message center for troubled families and enraged summer folk, who expect him to needle delinquent masons and carpenters. When we call Paris from the Mayor's, the circuits are filled with thready voices, undecipherable as phantoms, and we soon desist. No housecleaning zealots thump furniture over our heads. No cocktail parties and no television; once the dishes are done, we subside—or "bog," as Helen says—in our armchairs. Hers is Danish and supports the back scientifically; mine is fake Provençal, hideous but conducive to furtive dozing. Helen has learned not to twit me when the pages of the *Midi Libre* (which arrives in Barjaux a day late) tremble and droop in my hands.

Helen is reading Muriel Spark. She remains a metropolitan and secretly covets the Mayor's television. She misses her problem children too: the lame ducks of the Aid Society in Paris and the patients at the American Hospital. In Barjaux there are no study groups and no museums to befriend. The hours are less crowded than in the city, where chores take longer and bristle with confrontations and triumphs.

This summer I am reading Shakespeare, which I could never do in Paris or New York. Every night I take down the huge Rockwell Kent edition ("Doze with that one," Helen says, "and it will fall and kill you") from a niche in the stones, where scorpions (ours have a taste for ink and bindings) congregate in summer. I slog my way through *Henry VI* and whiz through *Henry IV* and *Othello* and *Troilus and Cressida.* The pentameters roll easily, with the river whispering down below, or the hooting of an owl to raise the hackles on my neck. The baying of watchdogs and the shouts from the bowling ground fuse into the voices of Cyprus or Eastcheap, or the clashes of the Grecian camp. When I tear myself away from that swarming universe and go to stand on our terrace, the stars of Troilus's farewell burn above me. Or two cats, graymalkins out of *Macbeth*, stalk the garden: round and round, along the wall, across the terrace, through the shadows in M. Gevaudan's garden, and back to the wall. Suddenly they break off their patrol and leap into the gap where we keep our cement faun: with a whisk of their tails, they vanish like the weird sisters.

August, with its blunting heat, has come again; the pebbles of the river bottom are drying; the grapes are swelling in the vineyards. And Eleanor has arrived. She is alone, but she hasn't brought her nine-by-five cards. Her long hair has lost its sheen.

"You look tired, dear," Helen says. "And thin. You need rest."

Eleanor's face darkens, but it's her first night: she takes refuge in mockery. "Scribble, scribble: it's hard work, you know. Not like you two—Provençal song and sunburnt mirth. I'm an ink-stained drudge."

Eleanor stifles in the attic, which we have turned over to her with Chinese apologies. Even in a West End walk-up, one has a toilet of one's own and a rattly air conditioner, not a pitcher and slop jar. "I had no idea the house was designed for elves." And then she adds quickly, "But it's really very cute. Really."

Though she scorns to be explicit, we know that Eleanor is waiting to see whether her flight will shake things up with Fred. Like a Dharma bum, Fred has taken to the road, with two other sculptors and assorted girls from SoHo. He is heading for California, leaving Eleanor to stew over Lamartine in the N.Y.U. Library. But this time, Patient Griselda has pulled a fast one.

For Eleanor the high point of the day is not the afternoon descent to the swimming hole or the evening walks on the herb-perfumed moor. What she waits for is the shrill horn of the postman as he zigzags up to Barjaux. Her hair swings bravely and her face lifts to the light as she climbs the steps to the daily conclave in the square. She greets the villagers more elegantly than we do, although alone with us she mimics their southern accents: *"Rieng pour toi dang le posta?"*

And alas, there is nothing. As she shuffles through the envelopes, separating personal mail from magazines and bills, her eyes cloud. We all go back down the steps in silence. Raymond, who has finally got his leave, stands by his motorbike, trying to look military; his *"Bonjour,* mademoiselle" gets only a curt nod. My toes curl for him: he isn't accustomed, as we are, to the Siberian exterior of Eleanor's warmth.

For all the rigors of military service, Raymond looks a bit whey-faced. When the villagers discover that he deserts the bowling ground to visit Saint-Genest, they warn him against the girls of the town, drawing on images from local fauna and flora: "Watch out for the goats! Don't wear down the walnuts!" Raymond grins darkly at the exploits they attribute to him. But Mme. Cayrol has tempered his relish for Eleanor by telling him that he is confronting a *docteur-ès-lettres*. So our daughter is not invited to mount the motorbike. She affects to be greatly relieved.

"I'm not a cradle snatcher," she tells us. "I'm saving that for my desperate forties." She finds Raymond absurd, but I can see that he reminds her of Fred. "Always on the go-go-go. Keep whirling; land running. The merry-go-round makes me sick. How can you ever stop to sit and think?"

"You might try here," Helen says. "Plenty of time to sit." She looks sideways at me. "In Barjaux you can think standing up."

The other city slicker gives her a grimace of complicity. "It's not what you'd call a jumping town, is it? Except for the dogs maybe. And those damned scorpions."

"Scorpions don't jump," I remind her sharply. "They scuttle."

"Lucky for us! I got another one last night in the bookcase. With my slipper."

"Bravo! But be careful. Lay off the spiders: they're good luck. And the crickets, of course."

Helen snorts. "Spiders! Crickets! Why don't you team up with Eulalie Douarnez? You could get out some new potions." And then she adds, "I wonder what those scorpions are after anyway. Maybe they migrate for the same stupid reasons we do."

Eleanor gives her a smile that makes me shiver. "Not for love, that's for sure. They're smarter than we are."

A water shortage hits us: the river dwindles to a clay-colored trickle and the faucets hawk up air. M. Gevaudan takes heroic measures: through Party connections in Nîmes he arranges the visit of a cistern truck, and we all go on rations. "Emergency," he tells us, beaming across the fence. "And not a drop for the campers."

Eleanor says "Tut tut" and quotes Marxist scripture: "To each according to his need."

The Mayor smiles sourly. *"Ils m'emmerdent, les campeurs."*

His revolutionary charms don't turn Eleanor on: he is too strong for her and needs no protective net. But they like to sharpen their knives on each other. Eleanor leans against the fence; he looks up from his tomato plants, one eyebrow magisterially cocked, beard bristling like that of Raphael's Saint Peter, and launches into French politics. Giscard and Mitterand are pinned and dissected, and then Carter and even Brezhnev. The schoolmistress joins them, and sometimes Raymond wanders into the garden with his fishing rods. The presence of the Right eggs the others into conspiracy to shock him. Their talk grows hotter and wilder as the sun declines in the blushing sky: religion, nationalism, property, marriage—the exploded ruins of faith and empire fall in showers about their ears.

Finally M. Gevaudan adjourns the meeting to the Mickey Bar. "Rather fun," Eleanor tells us next day. "Everyone pickled and talking at once. Southerners are full of talk, and that's about it. Except for sex, of course."

The Mayor tells us solemnly that our daughter is very intelligent. He asks whether she is our sole heir.

I jump. Is this the cloven hoof of land hunger under the Marxist robe? But when I tell him that Eleanor's interests are urban, he dries up like the river. He is only thinking of the future of his subjects: what will become of our property?

With Mme. Cayrol, Eleanor gets off on the right foot by complimenting her on the *belles de nuit* that open into a riot of red and yellow in an old washtub near her gate.

"You speak our language well, mademoiselle."

"You are too indulgent, madame."

"Indulgent? Me?" She shoots me a look. "Ask your father. Or my grandson, to whom I give so many free lectures."

"Raymond listens very little to advice from women, I think."

I gape at this, but our neighbor holds her own. "Not even from a *docteur-ès-lettres*?" She winks at me.

"Least of all, madame," Eleanor says cheerfully.

"But at his age, that's natural—as natural as bad advice from the old. And this month he is busy with the trout. Gamebirds and fish are always of interest, you know."

"Easier victims than we, madame."

"I wonder. Less of a nuisance anyway." Mme. Cayrol must be thinking of the schoolmistress.

"Well," says Eleanor, who must be thinking of Fred, "all sportsmen are a bit unfair, aren't they?"

Mme. Cayrol chortles, pressing gnarled fingers to her cheeks. "Ah, *pour cela,* mademoiselle. That's the least one can say."

After that the attachment between them is unbreakable.

The challenge of Eleanor's visit comes not from Raymond but from his brother. Released from the asylum, Étienne appears with his father in the last days of August. The villagers are putting in long hours in the vineyards, with watchful eyes on stray clouds, and the summer folk, incited by the waning arc of the sun, are polishing off social obligations.

"We must have a cocktail party," Helen says.

"Don't use that term around here."

But Helen has already drafted her decree. "We can ask the Mayor and his brother. The Parkinsons, of course. Maybe the Parisians who've opened the restaurant down by the bridge."

"What about our neighbors?"

Helen shakes her head. "Raymond and his father will be out on the moor with their shotguns, and Mme. Cayrol wouldn't leave the house in charge of Étienne. She never goes out anyway except on Bastille Day."

The Parkinsons arrive first from the other mountain, trailing a cloud of sons and daughters and grandchildren. The lilting British voices set off a paroxysm of yapping from Coca and her colleagues, and we watch anxiously as the picture hats come bobbing up the steps. The Mayor comes next, resplendent but uncomfortable in coat and tricolor tie.

The day is hot, and we bring Pastis and Scotch and what the younger Parkinsons call "small eats" out on the terrace in full view of passers-by. Suddenly we hear the creaking of Mme. Cayrol's gate. To our un-Christian consternation, Étienne ventures down the steps and into our garden; his black eyes burn with thirst for company. The Mayor and his brother look at each other, and then at Helen and me.

We call out to Étienne, and he climbs up to our terrace in a trance of diffidence. He is on parole from the asylum and can't drink, but Helen fetches him a coke. He holds it before his long-chinned face as if it were a chalice, and then goes to sit on the railing between Eleanor, whom he has recognized, and the Parkinson's youngest daughter Evelina, a sweet-faced girl with braids, who has just come back from a year of social work in Nigeria. Étienne begins to chatter as though he had downed several martinis. His French has specks of patois in it, like flour in gravy, and he rattles along to cover his stammer. The girls turn toward him, their behinds bulging over the stone ledge. They nod and sip and nod, interjecting syllables ("*Tiens!*" "*Dites donc!*") into the torrent of words, from which an occasional boulder of meaning—something about the *pétanque* matches or the wine harvest—rears up and then is submerged.

Presently we hear Mme. Cayrol piping shrilly, like Tristan's shepherd, from her garden. There is panic in her voice until Helen calls out, "We're all here, madame." She shuffles out in her bedroom slippers; when she sees Étienne, she presses a hand to her heart and gives a long sigh. She declines to join us but waits patiently outside her gate.

Étienne's pleasure has been cut off as if by the turn of a faucet. He shakes his head when we urge him to stay. Slowly he gets up from the railing, bows to the two girls and to Helen, and then his V-shaped mouth opens in an appalling giggle. When he has gone tit-tupping down our steps, I turn to the girls: "You both saved the day." Evelina's peaches-and-cream cheeks are suffused: "He was really rather sweet—like a Nigerian." Eleanor laughs: "You know, Dad, we understood nothing, not a single word." The Mayor, who has been experimenting politely with our Scotch, raises his glass to the girls.

After a minute, Evelina says shyly, "I say, was he perhaps a bit crackers?"

That night we hear footsteps in the attic, and then muffled weeping. Helen slips out from under the sheet and opens our bedroom door. When it gives out its usual high-pitched cry, the weeping stops. Helen stands poised, a billowy shape against the nightlight. But there is no sound, and she creeps back to bed, leaving the door open. "We absolutely must remember to oil that damned door," she says, as she has said every summer.

In the morning Eleanor, a little puffy around the eyes, announces briskly that she is off for Montpellier to look up friends from the Sorbonne, and then back to New York. "It's nice and peaceful here." She looks into the middle distance over my shoulder. "But you know how it is with me." She manages a smile. "Always on the prowl."

Helen and I babble in relays: we understand; next year more excitement; the Parkinson's secret swimming hole; concerts in the courtyard of the "château"; the centenary of Stevenson's travels.

Eleanor tries to refuse the check I press on her, but Helen makes her take it. Her eyes fill, she sniffles, and then goes next door to say goodbye to Mme. Cayrol and Raymond and Étienne. I escape down the village steps and back out the Renault.

Helen and I are driving back from the bus station in Saint-Genest when she breaks our silence to tell me that Eleanor is pregnant.

A few mornings later, when Helen has gone off to gather lavender, I hear the click of our gate, and Mme. Cayrol's gray head, with its bald spot, appears below the terrace wall.

I shout through the open window: *"Bonjour*, madame!" The visit has interrupted *The Winter's Tale*, but I am not really unhappy to leave Hermione and the woes of childbirth. "Come in, madame. Please."

The fingers that clutch at the railing are lumped with arthritis. In her other hand, Mme. Cayrol holds a tiny bottle. *"Voici,"* she says, panting. "They are *belles de nuit*. Try them in that shady patch under your wall." Inside the bottle are black seeds, pointed like cloves.

"You are too kind, madame. I'm sure you know how much we all admire yours."

On the terrace the wasps swarm around the sicky-sweet apéritifs to which Barjaux women are partial, so I persuade Mme. Cayrol to come into our *"living."* She admires the oak dining table, whose surface is pitted by two centuries in mountain kitchens, but I can see that her approval does not extend to the wispy-legged horses in the Dufy poster above the table. What really impresses her is our electric wiring: the stone walls being impenetrable, Hippolyte Barnouin simply fastened the gray cables with black staples to the vaults that top off the whitewashed walls.

"Tiens!" Mme. Cayrol peers upward. "It's like those striped arches in the basilica at Albi. Who did that for you?"

"Hippolyte Barnouin, madame."

"Very droll: I might have known. *Une fine mouche,* that Hippolyte."

"Yes, Hippolyte is very clever."

This sounds patronizing; Mme. Cayrol draws in a little. She tells me with dignity that clever artisans abound "in our villages." She lowers herself cautiously into the functional chair, but refuses an offer of Pastis, finally consenting to try a 7-Up—"*pour vous faire plaisir,* monsieur." She twitches her faded blue skirt around her knees; her brown eyes, flecked with cataract, gaze myopically at me. "*Eh bien, nos jeunes sont bien partis, n'est-ce pas?*" Her intonation has the meridional grace, strong on the final *e*'s. I am listening to a Roman matron, I feel: perhaps to the mother of absent Coriolanus.

"Yes, ours has left, madame. Your grandsons also?"

"Raymond went back to camp yesterday. And then he will return to Paris. After these visits he always seems so much farther away."

No need to tell her I understand: distances in scattered families mount with age in geometric progression. "You must miss him."

"Yes, monsieur, I miss him." She pauses for an instant. "I miss both my grandsons." She fidgets, looking for a new gambit. "We are close neighbors now, monsieur."

"Very. I hope we don't disturb you."

"On the contrary, monsieur. I am happier since you have come to Barjaux." She gives me a toothless smile and tells me that when Hippolyte installed our attic stairs, his drill went through the wall into her kitchen cupboard. "When I went to get supper, I found dust all over my dishes. And I could see light: it came from your windows."

"Hippolyte never told me a thing."

"He was embarrassed. But the next day he patched up the hole. In a way, I was sorry." She beams and twists her fingers together. "We are like that, you know: all tied up together. But that's as it should be, isn't it?"

"Of course."

She drains her 7-Up with a clicking noise and pulls herself to her feet. "I must water my flowers."

"We'll put in the *belles de nuit* this evening. Helen will appreciate your thinking of us."

"It is I who thank you, monsieur, and especially your dear daughter who has been so kind. But as she has left us—"

"Don't worry, madame. We'll tell her when we write."

"She gives great pleasure, your daughter, to everyone she talks with." Mme. Cayrol hobbles toward the door, turning shyly with her hand on the knob. "I only hope, monsieur, that God will send her greater happiness."

It is not the first time—nor the last, I am sure—that I am startled by Mme. Cayrol's perceptions.

The next day Helen and I stop at Mme. Cayrol's gate on our way up the hill with the garbage. She receives us in her garden, where she is taking the sun; she probably hesitates to ask the Americans, with their flush toilet and electric lights, into her house. So we stand there with our plastic bags—it makes an odd context for a call—and she hits us with the latest gossip.

"Mademoiselle Claire has announced her engagement."

"The schoolmistress?" Helen is astounded. "To M. Gevaudan, I suppose."

"Ah, no," says Mme. Cayrol with relish. "It's not the Mayor. It's our handsome mason."

"Hippolyte?"

"Ah, that Hippolyte! One can see he doesn't spend all his time on the rooftops. I told you he was a sly one."

"He has so many girls that we lost track. But so did the Mayor."

"I am told the bride is pregnant." Mme. Cayrol smiles wickedly: she must be relieved it isn't Raymond. "What a treat for her pupils! Let us hope that Eulalie Douarnez doesn't put a spell on her."

Helen laughs, but I wince. As the weeks pass with no word from New York, I find that an osmosis of village superstition has crept up on me. I keep running into Eulalie: she watches me from behind the grill of the ruin where she and Amédée nurse their poverty. When I greet her, she regales me with her exploits in a thick Languedoc accent: some gibberish about bringing back a faithless wife from Avignon.

"How did you manage that, madame?"

Her mouth puckers. "Relics, monsieur, from the bedroom. Hair, toenails, threads from the sheets. I pound them with basil and ewe's milk—but I mustn't tell you the amounts."

"Of course not," I say, as though I were a professional too.

"The faithful one spits in it and keeps it nearby. And the other one returns. *Voilà!*"

I may smile at the notion of relics from Fred, but I find myself picking up pins and skipping even-numbered steps on the hill. I say nothing to Helen, but she is onto me. Like many people without superstitions, she has second sight for four-leaf clovers, which she hands over to me during our walks. "Maybe they will help with the thesis," she says.

Marxist schoolmarm as ever, Mlle. Claire persuades Hippolyte to do without the religious service. So we all gather at the Mairie, across from the ignored church, and M. Gevaudan, draped in his tricolor sash, drones his way sadly through the banalities of the Republic's wedding service. Then we drift down to his garden for a *vin d'honneur*. The Gevaudan brothers pour Pastis and take turns with the camera, while the women hand around curling sandwiches.

"No sacrament, no procession," Mme. Cayrol says. Usually she keeps her counsel, but today she is vehement. "Nothing, nothing. Just a convenience of administration."

"Everyone looks happy anyway," Helen says. She nods toward the pergola, where the bride, who has wound artificial orange blossoms into her stiff hair, beams up at the groom. Hippolyte's blue eyes shift uneasily as he watches old girlfriends, and drinking companions, but he straightens up when Cuquemelle, with his albino thatch trimmed to honor his colleague, proposes a toast.

Madame Cayrol sinks down on a shady bench. "Happiness, madame, is rather insipid at times—like that sparkling cider that goes flat before you can get it to your mouth. Grief is stronger stuff in the long run." She pulls her purple shawl around her. "Monsieur, it would be most kind of you to fetch me a glass of wine."

Later we learn from the Mayor that our neighbor has had a call from Nîmes that morning. Étienne has slashed his wrists. He botched it, and his father found him in time, but he has been sent back to the hospital in Uzès.

One evening in September, while Helen is chuckling over *The Prime of Miss Jean Brodie* and I am nodding behind the *Midi Libre*, we hear rapid footsteps on our terrace and then a rapping on the windowpane. It is the Mayor. He is panting a bit, and when I ask him in, he shakes his head and says hoarsely, "A call for you. New York, I think."

Helen jumps up, overturning a coffee cup. Mechanically she stoops to pick it up. We don't have to look at each other to tune in the same images. It's five weeks since Eleanor left us. We've kidded ourselves that silence is a better sign than the frequent letters that spell loneliness. But now we see the wheels of a bus, the stealthy climb of a rapist in the walk-up. Or we hear the hooting of an ambulance on Columbus Avenue.

We follow M. Gevaudan across his garden and into his kitchen, where the telephone receiver, abandoned on the oilcloth among the dishes, squawks in competition with the television. A hanging bulb, moved by the night breeze, casts our swaying shadows on the wall. The Mayor punches off the television and rousts Coca out of the armchair. Reluctantly she follows him on stilt legs to the porch, where he takes her like a child to be protected from the disasters of grown-ups. I pick up the phone with sweating fingers; Helen listens on the earpiece.

A thin voice cries, "Allo, allo!" Then an electronic screech, and I hear Fred: "Where the hell are they anyway?"

"Fred!" I shout. "It's me. Where's Eleanor?"

"We've been trying to get you all afternoon."

"It's night here." (As though that made any difference.) "Is anything wrong? Is Eleanor all right?"

"She's fine. We have news for you." The syllables come burbling, as though from the depths of the sea. "Better for her to tell you herself, I guess."

Eleanor wastes no costly minutes: "We're getting married, Dad."

"Married!"

"That's right. In November."

"No kidding!" It's all I can find to say. "No kidding."

Eleanor's laugh is farther away than New York: a ghost cutting a caper. "Why would I kid you, Dad, on this solemn occasion?"

The blood returns to my cheeks. Helen grabs the phone, thrusting the earpiece into my hand. "Ellio, it's the best news ever." (*Ellio!* She hasn't called her that since she was in rompers.) "All our love to both of you." Helen levels off just on the edge of tears. "And is everything all right?"

"Just fine, Mom—worse luck! Wedding dress by Lane-Bryant, I guess." Their euphemisms bounce through the indifferent ionosphere. "But that's months away."

"We're dying to see you both."

"We don't plan to be married by M. Gevaudan." Eleanor's crust betrays just a crackle of anxiety. "We kind of wondered if you'd want to come all that way."

"Of course we're coming. What about Fred's parents?"

"We called you first." A pause. "Anyway, you remember there's only Fred's mother. In Chicago."

Helen raises an eyebrow at me. I push out of my mind the thought of our savings passbook. "Let me talk to Fred," Helen says.

"Hello, Mom." Fred brings it out queasily but without mockery. My heart warms: I see him in levis and a cutaway, his granny glasses misting over as he slices into the wedding cake.

We all blather on at the same time until Eleanor cuts in: "This is costing us bottles and bottles. Let's save it for drear November. Lots of love. To Mme. Cayrol too, and both the boys: Étienne especially."

Grandchildren: I shiver a little. Helen just says "Loads of love" and, as though handling an heirloom, puts the receiver on its cradle. A faint ding-ding, and we are back in the hush of Barjaux.

When he hears our news, the Mayor's eyes light as we have seen them do for other victories in Barjaux: a winning *pétanque* team, a house restored, better news of Étienne Cayrol, a sock in the Socialists' eye at elections. He takes down the Pastis, and the three of us sit silent, watching the milky clouds form in our glasses amid the ruins of his supper. Coca wags her tail and looks wistfully at the armchair.

When he clinks glasses with us, M. Gevaudan says, "I wish they could be here." His voice is filled with luminous sadness. Even assembled under the sign of love, each of us is alone, and no one more than the Mayor of our village.

As we climb back toward our lighted windows, I know that we have taken our first step on the road that leads away from Barjaux.

One night as I watch the autumn moon rising, orange and immense beyond the steeple, the log railing on our terrace crumbles under my arms and I barely escape pitching into the garden. When the first rains finally arrive, a tile comes loose from our roof, and the attic, empty now, begins to smell of mildew. Hippolyte and Cuquemelle are summoned to the rescue, but I feel uneasy: are these warnings to defectors?

The blue tents of the campers vanish, and one by one the summer folk close their shutters, but still we linger. M. Gevaudan tells us, with a wink, that if we last out October, he will proclaim us natives and reserve us a place on the village council.

The scorpions are in retreat too: one of them scurries for cover when I reach for the Shakespeare, then freezes on the whitewashed wall, venomous tail erect, as though immobility would make him invisible. I know that illusion: I am tempted to leave him as my hostage to borrowed time. But in the end I crack him sharply with my bedroom slipper. Helen gives a little cry. "It's not a cricket," I tell her.

Crickets and clovers—none of the auguries brings much luck to Marguerite Cayrol.

On a day of Indian summer, she goes to visit a friend across the river, who is known as the goat-lady because of her big herd of black-and-tans. The goat-lady's house is way off the main road, so that instead of taking the big bridge that bears her husband's name, Mme. Cayrol has to ford the river on stepping stones. Scorning offers of escort, she sets off, clutching a knobby cane and a bag of figs. We imagine her and the goat-lady sipping Bartissol and catching up on gossip: Hippolyte's marriage, followed by the succulent catalogue of his conquests; the wine harvest; M. Gevaudan's politics; the feud between the *garde-champêtre* and the nudist campers. We are sure that the Americans and their daughter are not exempted.

As we reconstruct the sequel, she starts back alone in the twilight, carrying a bag of goat cheeses. She has just reached the last stepping stone when her foot slips: she falls full length and smashes her hip. A goatherd, stumbling home from the Mickey Bar, finds her on the bank, staring up at the stars and hooting faintly, like an owl fallen from its nest. He goes back for the Mayor.

M. Gevaudan phones to Saint-Genest for an ambulance and mobilizes his brother and me and the carpenter, who rigs up a stretcher from an old door. With Cuquemelle's poll glinting in the moonlight like a beacon, we descend to the river. Gently the Gevaudan brothers roll Mme. Cayrol onto the door. She cries out once— *"Ah mon dieu, mon dieu!"*—and then subsides into faint moaning. Cuquemelle rescues the bag of cheeses. "She is not much of a load, *la Marguerite*," the Mayor says. But we go slowly, slowly up the village steps.

Near the church the blue light of the ambulance is whirling. An attendant, who looks about fifteen to me, slouches against the wall of the parvis, puffing on a cigar. The neighbors gather; Helen has come out with a shawl thrown over her bathrobe. She fishes the house keys from Mme. Cayrol's pocket and beckons to Claire Barnouin.

"Bring the crucifix," Mme Cayrol whispers. "It's at the head of the bed. And the bottle of *eau de mélisse*."

We all stand watching the light of the kerosene lamp flickering along from room to room behind the shutters. Later Helen tells me that the bedroom contains only a brass bed, a washstand, and a walnut armoire full of black dresses.

The attendant gives Mme. Cayrol a shot, and when the two women return, she is enjoying the first pleasure of morphine. She keeps repeating that her name is Marguerite. But no drug can dull the sudden pangs of dependence. "Don't go to so much trouble," she says to everyone and no one. *"Et appelez-moi Marguerite."*

"No trouble, Madame Marguerite," M. Gevaudan tells her. After a quick whisper with the rest of us, he decides to stay in the village in case official help is needed. He deputizes Hippolyte as escort.

Mme. Cayrol stretches out a broomstick arm, groping for Helen's neck. "You've really done too much, and Monsieur too." She raises her head. "And don't forget to give my love to your daughter. Tell her it's from your *drôle de voisine.*"

"Of course, Marguerite." Helen wipes her forehead, pecks her on the cheek. Then we slide her into the ambulance like a loaf into an oven. Hippolyte gives Mme. Claire a squeeze of the neck that translates, "Duty calls but keep the bed warm," and races down the steps to get his Deux-Chevaux. The ambulance trundles cautiously around the first hairpin and then picks up speed. Hippolyte's car comes darting after, side windows flapping. The firefly lights vanish in a rocky defile, only to reappear far below at the bridge. At the braying of the klaxon, we all draw together until this alien city noise has died away. The dogs prowl in circles around us. When a cloud floats black across the moon, the whisper of the river comes more clearly to us. The cloud moves on, and we break up and become just a lot of people going home.

At the end of the month, while we are crating up books and china, we hear the banging of shutters next door. It is Raymond, who has been sent to fetch some of his grandmother's effects. His mustachios have grown so long that he can curl them at the ends. He tells us that Mme. Cayrol is confined to a wheelchair in a rest home in Nîmes: she is not likely to climb the steps of Barjaux again. Her house, like ours, will be put up for sale. Raymond and his parents go to see her whenever they can, but not Étienne: no one knows whether he will ever leave the asylum.

We send our love and the last jar of the apricots from our tree. We conceal from Raymond that Amédée Douarnez, who can't tell flowers from pigweed, has ripped out all our *belles de nuit.* ("How could I help it," he says dismally, "if they won't come out until after dark?")

Raymond profits from his mission to join his hunting pals on the moor and in the *bal musette* at Saint-Genest. One night we hear giggles and faint cries through the stone wall, and the jingling of Mme. Cayrol's brass bedstead.

"Raymond has raided the valley."

"Men!" says Helen. "I've got a good mind to knock on the wall."

" 'No sooner had, past reason hated.' "

"What?"

"Just talking to myself. The pleasures of old age."

The agent has found us a buyer: a spit-and-polish colonel from Metz, Protestant and a whiz at *pétanque*, with a taciturn wife in a bucket hat. We couldn't have done better by the village. I swear M. Gevaudan to secrecy till we pass the word, but when people get ready to leave—whether it's a house or life itself—their wishes no longer matter. Once the deed is signed, our desertion is known all over the village. Now we grit our teeth for the farewells.

Fortunately the cold has speeded the diaspora of the other out-landers. The Mayor's brother and his wife and Cuquemelle drop in of their own accord. The Douarnezes do not appear; we shrink from intruding on their misery, and we don't want to hear Amédée apologize again for the flowers. Through the window I catch one glimpse of Eulalie shuffling down the steps, eyes fixed on the bowl in her hands, as though she were carrying the viaticum. I duck back before she sees me.

Raymond shouts *"Bon courage"* and roars off on his motorbike, with the rods of his faltboat slung over his shoulder, like arrows in a quiver. The shuttered windows of his grandmother's house remind me of closed eyes. The flowers dry into yellow and surrender their hold on the little parterre she had scooped out among the stones.

On our last Sunday, we go down to the Barnouins' house. Mme. Claire is peeling potatoes by the kitchen fire. When she gets up, we can see that her belly has begun to swell: the Marxist pedagogue looks a model of domesticity. Hippolyte is assembling cartridges in a scarlet harness that crisscrosses his chest. Regular meals are making him paunchy, and the faun's gleam has gone from his eye, snuffed out by the quieter comforts of the double bed.

We drink a glass of the new wine and talk of everything but departure: partridges, rabbits, the early frost, Mme. Cayrol. Hippolyte looks up from his gun, shaking his hair away from his eyes: "In America, will your house be of stone or of wood?"

"Neither," Helen tells him. "Concrete and steel. A building with hundreds of others in it."

"*Tiens!*" Hippolyte and Mme. Claire exchange pitying glances. And then it is time for the ritual sighs and good wishes for the journey and, on both sides, for the children.

As we climb the steps again, Mayor Gevaudan comes out on his porch, where the canopy of vines flutters crimson in the wind. Behind him we can see our windows blazing up in the sunset; this time the dormer holds the flame longer than usual, flashing toward the west minutes after the other panes have gone blank.

This is the hardest moment: at least it will be brief. M. Gevaudan takes my hand in both of his big ones (he is too shy to do this with Helen); his mouth opens, and nothing comes out. I wouldn't blame him if he said, "I knew you wouldn't stay the course."

But I have underestimated our mayor. His corkscrew beard trembles, and he brings out the words I know I shan't forget: "*Vous resterez tout près de notre coeur.*"

"Our heart." Helen looks at me; she has caught it too. And on that royal note, the foreign envoys take their departure.